THIS DIARY BELONGS TO:

Nikki J. Maxwell

PRIVATE & CONFIDENTIAL

If found, please return to ME for REWARD!

(NO SNOOPING ALLOWED!!!☹)

ALSO BY
Rachel Renée Russell

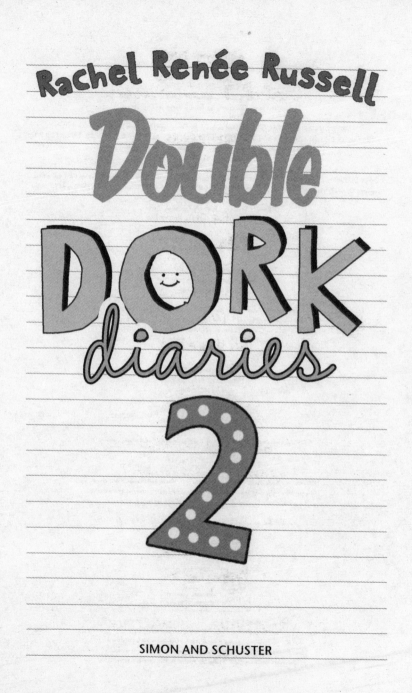

Rachel Renée Russell

Double
DORK
diaries
2

SIMON AND SCHUSTER

This edition published 2016
First published as an omnibus edition in Great Britain in 2013 by
Simon and Schuster UK Ltd,
A CBS COMPANY.

Simon & Schuster UK Ltd
1st Floor, 222 Gray's Inn Road, London WC1X 8HB

DORK DIARIES: POP STAR first published in Great Britain in 2011 by Simon and Schuster UK Ltd,
a CBS company. Originally published in 2011 in the USA as DORK DIARIES: TALES FROM A NOT-SO-TALENTED POP
STAR by Aladdin, an imprint of Simon & Schuster Children's Publishing Division,
1230 Avenue of Americas, New York.

DORK DIARIES: SKATING SENSATION first published in Great Britain in 2012 by Simon and Schuster UK Ltd, a CBS
company. Originally published as DORK DIARIES: TALES FROM A NOT-SO-GRACEFUL ICE PRINCESS in 2012 in the
USA by Aladdin, an imprint of
Simon & Schuster Children's Publishing Division,
1230 Avenue of Americas, New York.

Copyright © Rachel Renée Russell 2011 and 2012
Book design by Lisa Vega

13

Simon & Schuster UK Ltd
1st Floor, 222 Gray's Inn Road
London WC1X 8HB

Simon & Schuster Australia, Sydney
Simon & Schuster India, New Delhi

A CIP catalogue record for this book is available from the British Library.

ISBN 978-1-47111-673-5

Printed and bound by CPI Group (UK) Ltd, Croydon, CR0 4YY

www.simonandschuster.co.uk
www.simonandschuster.com.au

MIX
Paper from
responsible sources
FSC® C020471

Simon & Schuster UK Ltd are committed to sourcing paper
that is made from wood grown in sustainable forests and support the Forest
Stewardship Council, the leading international forest certification organisation.
Our books displaying the FSC logo are printed on FSC certified paper.

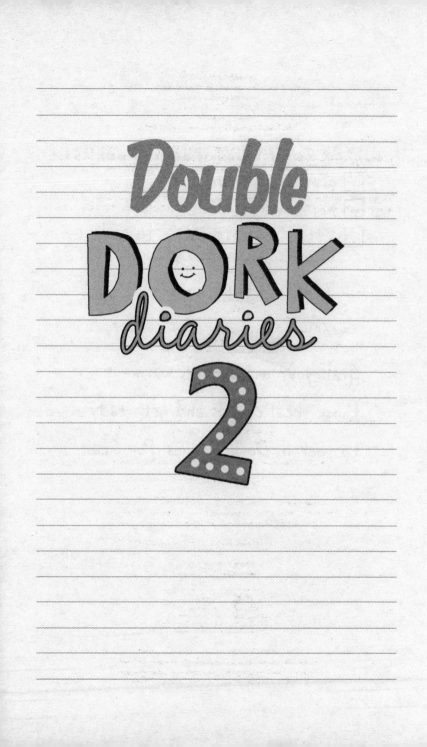

Nikki's Road to Stardom checklist

- ☑ Diva showdown
- ☑ BFF feud
- ☒ Talented entourage to back up VIP (Very Important Pop Star)

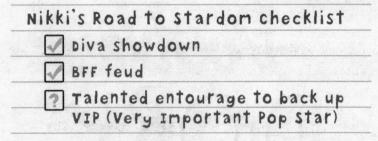

Grab your microphone, warm-up those vocal chords and get ready to rock in *Dork Diaries: Pop Star...*

OMG!

I think yesterday was probably the BEST day of my entire life ☺!!

Not only did I have a FABTASTIC time at the Halloween dance with my crush, Brandon, but I think he might actually like me! SQUEEEEEEEEEE!!!! ☺!!

By "like," I mean as a REALLY good friend.

Definitely NOT as a serious girlfriend or anything. I'm sure THAT would NEVER happen in a million years!

WHY? Mostly because I'm the biggest DORK in the entire school.

And with three spots, two left feet, one cruddy social life and zero popularity, I'm not exactly the type of girl who'll one day be crowned prom queen.

But thanks to my wicked case of CRUSH-ITIS, the slightly-goofy-blissfully-lovesick-shabby-chic style I'm currently rockin' would definitely put me in the running for . . .

PRINCESS OF THE DORKS!

It's just that I'm NOT a tag hag (also known as a totally obsessed fashion SNOB).

And I'm NOT hopelessly addicted to spending twice the gross national product of a small third-world country on the latest designer clothes, shoes, jewelry, and handbags, only to REFUSE to wear the stuff one month later because it's "like, OMG! Practically more ANCIENT than YESTERDAY!!"

UNLIKE some people I know. . .

"People" being shallow, self-centred girls like . . .

MACKENZIE HOLLISTER ☹!!

Calling MacKenzie a "mean girl" is an understatement. She's a RATTLESNAKE in pink plumping lip gloss and ankle boots.

But I'm NOT intimidated by her or anything. Like, how juvenile would THAT be?!

I constantly wonder how girls like MacKenzie always manage to be so . . . I don't know . . .

PERFECT.

I wish I had something that could magically transform ME into my perfect self.

It would have the amazing power of Cinderella's fairy godmother, be easy to use and be small enough to fit inside a bag or backpack.

Something like, I dunno, maybe . . .

MAXWELL'S ENCHANTED LIP GLOSS ☺!

My special lip gloss would make each and every girl look as beautiful on the OUTSIDE as she is on the INSIDE!

How COOL would THAT be?!

AVERAGE NICE GIRL (LIKE ME)

BEFORE
**ENCHANTED
LIP GLOSS**

(WE SEE A
NORMAL GIRL.)

AFTER
**ENCHANTED
LIP GLOSS**

(WE MAGICALLY SEE
MY INNER BEAUTY.)

☺!!

AVERAGE MEAN GIRL (LIKE MACKENZIE)

After spending hours studying the potential global impact of the Enchanted Lip Gloss phenomenon, I was shocked and amazed by my scientific findings:

Enchanted Lip Gloss does *NOT* look CUTE on EVERYONE! Too bad, MacKenzie ☺!!

Anyway, I really hope Brandon calls me today.

I would totally FREAK if he actually did. But I'm pretty sure he probably won't. Which, BTW, brings me to this VERY important question . . .

HOW ARE YOU SUPPOSED TO KNOW WHEN A GUY ACTUALLY LIKES YOU IF HE NEVER BOTHERS TO CALL???!!!

CRUSH IQ TEST: Carefully examine the following two pictures for sixty seconds. Can you spot the DIFFERENCE between them?

ANSWER: There is NO DIFFERENCE! These two dudes are IDENTICAL!

Which, unfortunately, means your crush basically IGNORES you whether he actually LIKES YOU or NOT!

ARRRGGGGHH!!!...

(That was me tearing my hair out in frustration!)

Lucky for me, my BFF Chloe is an expert on guys and romance. She learned everything she knows from reading all the latest teen magazines and novels.

And my other BFF Zoey is a human Wikipedia and a self-help guru. She's basically a fourteen-year-old Dr Phil in lip gloss and hoop earrings.

The three of us are going to meet at the mall tomorrow to shop for jeans. I can't wait to talk to them about all this guy stuff because, seriously, I don't have a CLUE!

SATURDAY, NOVEMBER 2

Can someone PLEASE tell me WHY my life is so horrifically PATHETIC ☹?!

Even when something *FINALLY* goes RIGHT, something else *ALWAYS* goes terribly WRONG!!!

My mom was supposed to be taking me to the mall today to hang out with Chloe and Zoey. So I was TOTALLY BUMMED when she told me I had to watch my bratty little six-year-old sister, Brianna, for forty-five minutes while she shopped for a new toaster ☹!

In spite of her cute little angelic face and pink sneakers, Brianna is actually a baby Tyrannosaurus rex. On STEROIDS!

There was no way I was going to hang out with my BFFs with HER tagging along.

So I told Chloe and Zoey I'd try to meet up with them as soon as my mom finished shopping.

I found a quiet, comfortable spot to chillax with my diary. Then I ordered Brianna to park her little butt right beside me on the bench and not move.

ME,
WATCHING BRIANNA
(SORT OF . . . .)

I hadn't taken my eyes off Brianna for more than a minute (or two or five) when I discovered she'd climbed into the mall fountain to hunt for coins!

Thank goodness that water was really shallow!

Then I made the mistake of asking Brianna what the heck she was doing in that fountain. She put her hands on her hips and glared at me impatiently.

"Can't you see it's an emergency?! A mean old witch has kidnapped Princess Sugar Plum. And Miss Penelope needs to get this money out of the water so we can buy a real, live baby unicorn from the grocery store and fly to save the princess!"

Hey, you ask a SILLY question, you get a SILLY answer!

I dragged her out of the fountain and made her toss back the big pile of coins she'd gathered.

Of course, Brianna was supermad at me for ruining her little treasure hunt.

So, to distract her, I suggested we take a little stroll through the food court to try to find some FREE food samples to snack on. YUMMY!

That's when Brianna started nagging me to take her to her favourite kiddie pizza joint, Queasy Cheesy.

I don't have the slightest idea why little kids love that place so much. It has these huge, stuffed, robotic animals that dance and sing off-key.

Personally, I think it's supercreepy the way their eyes roll around in their heads and their mouths are always out of sync with their voices.

Maybe it's just me, but WHO would actually want to EAT in a restaurant that has a six-foot-tall, mangy-looking RAT scampering around? I don't care that it sings "Happy Birthday" and gives out free balloons!

To me, the ONLY thing SCARIER was that evil clown who used to live under my bed when I was really little.

My parents always insisted he was just a figment of my imagination. But he was VERY real to ME!

BOO!

THE IMAGINARY EVIL CLOWN WHO LIVED UNDER MY BED

OMG! I was absolutely TERRIFIED he'd grab my ankles and pull me under my bed and I'd be STUCK there for, like, ETERNITY.

Thank goodness I'm older and more mature and NOT scared of silly, childish stuff like evil clowns.

Except maybe during thunderstorms on really dark nights when I see these strange shadows. . .

Anyway! I was like, "Sorry, Brianna! I don't have any money. We'll have to wait until Mum gets back."

"But I can pay for it!" Brianna whined. "With my baby unicorn money from that magical fountain. I'm a RICH people practically! I wanna go to QUEASY CHEESY! NOW!!"

That's when I noticed that all of Brianna's pockets were stuffed with coins from that fountain.

My little sister WASN'T "a rich people practically".

But she DID have enough loose change to buy us a medium sausage pizza with drinks.

WOO-HOO!! ☺!!

The pizza was actually pretty good! For Queasy Cheesy, anyway.

Just as we were finishing up our meal, a waitress pulled a random number out of a bowl and excitedly announced that the guests at table 7 were the "lucky ducks" she'd selected to come up onstage and sing the "I Luv Queasy Cheesy" theme song.

I was like, "Oh, CRUD!!" Brianna and I were sitting at table 7 ☹!!

There was just NO WAY I was going up on that stage in front of all those people to sing that stupid song. And I made that fact VERY clear to the nice waitress lady.

Of course, that's when Brianna got an attitude about the whole thing.

She actually threw a hissy fit right there in the restaurant and – get this – REFUSED TO PAY FOR OUR FOOD!!!!

OMG!

I had never been SO embarrassed in my life!

I totally panicked because all I had in my pocket was thirty-nine cents and some lint.

Money?!
Well, you're NOT going to believe this, but . . .
BUT . . .

But the superSCARY part was that Brianna's silly little prank was going to land us BOTH in JAIL!

And YES! I'm aware that doing prison time is the latest fad for all those spoiled young celebs.

You know the type. The infamous party girl/
model/actress who manages to become both an
ICON and an EX-CON before her twenty-first
birthday.

She truly believes she's above the law, because in
her little mind the only REAL CRIMES against
humanity are . . .

1. Fake designer purses
2. FRENEMIES
3. People with visible ear and nose hairs

So out of sheer desperation, I did what I had
to do.

Namely, perform the "I Luv Queasy Cheesy" song
with Brianna so she would pay for our meal.

Thank goodness the people there were mostly
parents and little kids. I didn't see anyone I knew
from my school.

Once we took the stage and I'd got past my feelings

19

of extreme embarrassment and mild nausea (which is probably why they call the place QUEASY Cheesy!), I had to admit the whole experience was actually kind of FUN!!

The crowd seemed to love us, so Brianna and I really

HAMMED IT UP!

We were getting down with a few Beyoncé dance moves, and the audience was cheering us on.

Then the most AWFUL and SHOCKING thing happened . . .

MACKENZIE HOLLISTER!

Apparently, she'd just arrived with HER little sister, Amanda, and her BFF, Jessica.

Jessica was pointing and laughing at me like I was the biggest joke since the interrupting cow.

And I totally FREAKED when I realized MacKenzie had her phone out and seemed to be taking a picture or something.

I grabbed Brianna and practically carried her off the stage.

"NOOO! Let go of me!" Brianna screamed. "The song isn't even over yet! We have to throw kisses to the crowd and—"

"Brianna! It's time to go!" I huffed, still out of breath. "Mom is probably waiting for us back at the fountain!"

But before we made it to the door, Amanda rushed over and shoved a pen and napkin into Brianna's hand. "I've NEVER met a real, live pop star before! Can I have your autograph?" she gushed.

Brianna beamed. "SURE! You can have it for FREE!

And I'll draw a picture of my real, live baby unicorn too! I can ride him if I want. He flies in the air!"

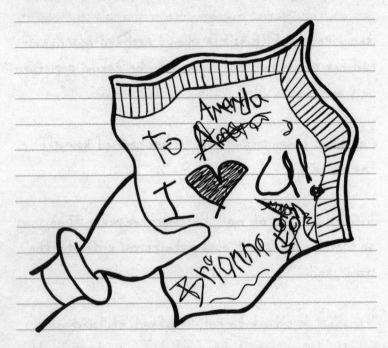

Amanda's eyes widened to the size of saucers. "YOU have a REAL baby unicorn?! Can I see it?!"

I could NOT believe Brianna was lying like that. I gave her a dirty look and she stuck her tongue out at me.

"Well, I don't have one just YET. But I'm gonna buy

it from the grocery store as soon as my mom comes back with our new toaster. 'Cause guess what?!
Some idiot poured orange juice in our old one and it exploded and blew up our house. KABOOM!!"

"Brianna!" I scolded. "Move it! RIGHT NOW!!"

Actually, I was just trying to get out of there before MacKenzie came over. But no such luck.

"OMG!! Nikki! You were hilarious!" MacKenzie shrieked. "You stunk worse than the boys' locker room!"

"Yeah, it took a lot of guts to get up there and humiliate yourself in front of the entire WORLD like that!" Jessica snorted.

I just rolled my eyes at both of them.

I knew I wasn't a professional singer or dancer, but the crowd seemed to like us. And since when had MacKenzie and Jessica become experts on talent?

"Oh, please! You two wouldn't recognize talent if it came up wearing a name tag, introduced itself, and slapped your face!" I blurted out.

MacKenzie and Jessica just glared at me. I think they were probably a little surprised because I usually just ignore them or say stuff inside my head that no one else can hear but me.

But there's only so much verbal abuse a person can take.

"And besides," I continued, "there aren't more than fifty people in here. I wouldn't call that the ENTIRE world."

"Well, it WILL BE when I post this on YouTube," MacKenzie said, sneering as she waved her camera right in my face. "Nikki Maxwell, LIVE at Queasy Cheesy!! And you can thank ME for launching your career as a NOT-so-talented pop star!"

Then MacKenzie and Jessica both laughed hysterically at her witty little joke.

26

I just stood there, stunned. Would MacKenzie actually do that to me?!

Something so . . . SINISTER and so . . . VILE?!

Suddenly my stomach felt really sick again and started making gurgling sounds like that angry chocolate fountain at MacKenzie's party.

Only it felt like I had just eaten a dirty sock and then washed it down with a large glass of room-temperature vinegar.

If I didn't get out of there fast, MacKenzie and Jessica were going to have a SECOND video to post on YouTube. One of me BARFING stale pizza and watered-down fruit punch all over their $300 designer jeans!

When we finally met up with Mom, she was surprised I was so anxious to go home.

I just told her I didn't feel so well and had decided not to go shopping with Chloe and Zoey after all.

So now I'm in my bedroom writing about all this and trying not to

FREAK OUT!

Because if MacKenzie posts that Queasy Cheesy video on YouTube . . .

OMG!!!

Somebody please DIAL 911 because I'm going to have a massive heart attack and DIE!!

SUNDAY, NOVEMBER 3

I was so depressed about what happened at Queasy Cheesy yesterday, I could barely drag myself out of bed this morning.

So I figured . . . why bother?!

I decided to just lie there STARING at the wall and SULKING.

For some reason, wallowing in a truckload of self-pity always makes me feel a lot better ☺!

I finally got up around noon and spent the rest of the day online checking YouTube. I was on there practically every ten minutes. I couldn't help it. It was like I was obsessed or something.

I was hoping MacKenzie had just been joking about posting that video.

She absolutely LOVES to torture me like that.

By 8:30 p.m. I'd come to the conclusion that the whole thing was just a nasty prank to FREAK me out. And it HAD!

MacKenzie is meaner than a junkyard dog and totally despises me. But thank goodness she hadn't gone THAT far!

I decided to check one last time before I went to bed and then forget about the whole thing. . .

It was official.

NIKKI MAXWELL,

LIVE AT QUEASY CHEESY

was now on YouTube for the

world's viewing pleasure!

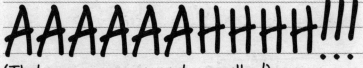

And it had already had seven views ☹!

I was DEVASTATED!

There was only one thing left for me to do. . .

AAAAAAAHHHHH!!!

(That was me screaming into my pillow!)

How am I going to face the kids at my school, knowing they're all secretly laughing at me behind my back?!

And what about Chloe, Zoey and Brandon?

They're the greatest friends ever.

I cringed at the thought of putting them through more of the DRAMAFEST that is my life.

I kept repeating one thing over and over in my head . . .

WHY ME?!

☹!!

MONDAY, NOVEMBER 4

There was NO WAY I was going to go to school today to face my public execution by video.

So I got up extra early to make a batch of my infamous Stay-Home-from-School Faux Vomit.

Unfortunately, that was NOT an option, because we were totally out of oatmeal. I was like, JUST GREAT ☹!!

When I finally arrived at school, I was expecting to be mercilessly teased, peppered with insults and bombarded with a never-ending supply of very lame Queasy Cheesy jokes.

But to my surprise, no one even mentioned that stupid video. THANK GOODNESS ☺!! Instead, the entire school was superexcited and buzzing about the upcoming annual Westchester Country Day talent show!

It's scheduled for Saturday, November 30th, and the judge this year is Trevor Chase, the famous producer of the new hit TV show *15 Minutes of Fame*. Turns out he went to WCD!

The prizes were supposed to be pretty good too, with first place being the chance to audition for a spot on his television show. How cool is THAT?!

So now Chloe, Zoey and I are TOTALLY psyched about the talent show!

We've already agreed to perform together. We just have to figure out what we're going to do. It's gonna be a BLAST for sure ☺!

I'd give anything to be a rich and famous singing sensation!

WHY?

Because when Nikki Maxwell the WCD STUDENT is WEIRD, RUDE, SLOPPY and CRAZY, everyone HATES her. She's called a LOSER ☹!

However, when Nikki Maxwell the POP STAR is WEIRD, RUDE, SLOPPY and CRAZY, she gets mobbed by fans, paid millions of dollars and everyone LOVES her. She's called a LEGEND ☺!

ME, AS A NOT-SO-TALENTED
POP PRINCESS LEGEND

My hot dog is so groovy! *Burp!* But hold the mustard, please, 'cause I'd rather have my hot dog with peanut butter and cheese!

We ♥ You!

Anyway, I SAW BRANDON IN BIOLOGY TODAY!! SQUEEEEEEEEEEEEE ☺!!

Well, actually, I see Brandon in biology *EVERY DAY*. But today was superspecial because it was the first time I've seen him since the DANCE!!

He told me (*AGAIN*) how much he enjoyed hanging out with me! SQUEEEEEEEEEEEE ☺!!

And get this!! He said we should consider sitting together at lunch to study for our future biology tests!!! I blushed profusely and suggested that we start studying for the next test ASAP.

Like . . . TOMORROW! ☺!!

Mostly because I'm VERY serious about my studies. Especially my BIOLOGY tests!

ME, STUDIOUSLY STUDYING FOR ALL MY CLASSES AT THE SAME TIME!!

But Brandon said he couldn't sit with me at lunch for the next couple weeks because his editor has assigned him to train a new photographer for the school newspaper.

I smiled at him and was like, "Um . . . Okay! Sure."

But deep down inside I was a little disappointed.

I started worrying that maybe he was just making up a lame excuse because he didn't want to hang out with me after all.

So I decided to talk to Chloe and Zoey about it.

Chloe said for me not to worry because Brandon was the one who came up with the whole sitting-together-at-lunch thing. Which meant he was ready to take our relationship to the next level. And Zoey totally agreed.

SQUEEEEEEE ☺!

OMG! I almost forgot! Now I have ONE more thing

to lie awake nights worrying about. There were at least a dozen ants crawling around in biology today!

MacKenzie made a big fuss about getting ant germs until our teacher told her that if she didn't sit down and finish her lab report, her grade was going to be A LOT nastier than any ant germs.

But what if the problem gets worse?! This could turn into a major disaster! My teacher could complain to the janitor, the janitor could complain to the secretary, the secretary could complain to the principal and the principal could complain to . . .

MY DAD, THE SCHOOL EXTERMINATOR ☹!!!

MUST. NOT. PANIC!! Breathe in, breathe out!

ANYWAY, before I so rudely interrupted myself,

I was about to say that Chloe and Zoey think Brandon might actually like me!

And those little ants seem to think so TOO!

MacKenzie is even more EVIL than I imagined!

I was wondering why she had gone through the trouble of recording that video of me at Queasy Cheesy and posting it on YouTube, only to keep it a big SECRET!

It made no sense WHATSOEVER! But NOW I know why she did it.

I was at my locker jotting down ideas for the talent show when I was rudely interrupted.

"What's up, Nikki! I've got some superEXCITING news to tell you, HON. . . !!"

I could NOT believe MacKenzie had the nerve to come up to me acting all friendly like she hadn't just tried to DESTROY MY LIFE a mere three days ago!

"I'm putting together a group for the talent show,

and I'm looking for supertalented dancers with real star power. Here's all the info."

Then she smiled really big, batted her superlong lashes, and shoved a piece of paper right in my face. . .

ME

I squinted and tried to read it.

But I was having a really hard time because she dangled it in front of my eyes and started swinging it back and forth.

And back and forth.

And back and forth.

Like she was trying to HYPNOTIZE me to do her EVIL BIDDING or something!

I knew right then and there she was up to no good.

It took every ounce of my strength NOT to be completely mesmerized by the brilliant radiance of her awesome, yet sickening, perfection.

Finally I just snatched the paper from her and read it.

ARE YOU CUTE, COOL & TALENTED?

Do you love to dance?

If so, join

MAC'S MANIACS

A dance group choreographed by MacKenzie Hollister

First performance will be at the WCD talent show.

Practice dates to be announced

I had a REALLY bad feeling about that girl and her little dance-group thing.

Why would she want ME?!

Especially after Chloe, Zoey, and I got that D
on our Ballet of the Zombies dance routine
in gym.

Then there was that other small issue . . .

SHE HATES MY GUTS!!

And after her very public and humiliating defeat at
the art competition, I was sure she was hatching a
diabolical plan to win the talent show.

Unless, after seeing me perform at Queasy Cheesy,
MacKenzie had suddenly realized I was supertalented,
with huge star power?

Maybe she wanted me ON her team so she wouldn't
have to compete AGAINST me.

The whole concept kind of blew my mind.

That's when I started thinking that working with

MacKenzie on her dance group might allow us to put aside our differences and *finally* become friends.

It would be nice NOT having to put up with her verbal abuse or worry about her blabbing my personal business.

I even tried to convince myself that hanging out with MacKenzie wouldn't be so bad.

Once I got used to her abrasive personality.

And her over-inflated ego.

And her addiction to lip gloss.

And the fact that she has the IQ of a plastic houseplant.

I even imagined myself doing the kind of stuff I'd overheard the CCP (Cute, Cool & Popular) clique bragging about.

Like lounging on the beach at MacKenzie's summer home in the Hamptons.

ME, IN A
SUPERCUTE SWIMSUIT,
LOUNGING ON THE
BEACH AT MACKENZIE'S
SUMMER HOME!!

I'd definitely invite my friends to MY summer home
in the Hamptons! If I had one. . .

Finally I made up my mind to give her a chance.

Chloe, Zoey and I were going to have a blast dancing
onstage together in MacKenzie's group.

49

It would be just like our old Ballet of the Zombies days, only BETTER! I got a really warm and fuzzy feeling inside just thinking about it ☺!!

MacKenzie pulled out her new lip gloss, Decadent Dancing Diva Delight, applied a fresh layer, and stared at me with her icy blue eyes.

"So, Nikki . . . if you know any supertalented dancers with star power, like, um . . . CHLOE and ZOEY, just give 'em this flyer, okay?"

My brain was like, "What the . . . ?!! Did she just say 'Chloe and Zoey'?!"

Apparently, the little blonde-haired weasel wanted ONLY Chloe and Zoey in her dance group and not ME!

Hey, I'd be the FIRST to admit that Chloe and Zoey were supertalented dancers, probably two of the best in the school.

But what did MacKenzie think I was? CHOPPED LIVER?! REFRIED BEANS?!!

It felt like she had just slapped me across the face. With a steel pipe or something.

"Um . . . sure," I muttered. "I'll tell Chloe and Zoey. But just so you know, the three of us were already planning on doing something for the talent show together."

"Well, you're going to have to CHANGE your PLANS, then! I really want that audition for *15 Minutes of Fame*. And if Chloe and Zoey perform with ME instead of a no-talent LOSER like YOU, it'll be a slam dunk for me to take first place."

I could NOT believe MacKenzie was talking smack right to my face like that.

"GIRL, PUH-LEEZE!" I said, doing one of those Tyra Banks neck-roll thingies that I'd practised in the mirror for hours. "You must be delusional or something. Or maybe your hair clips are so tight, they're cutting off the oxygen to your brain. In spite of what those voices in your head are telling you, we're NOT your little monsters!

I suggest you go find some other people to be your puppets!"

MACKENZIE
AS A
PUPPETEER →

ZOEY ↓

ME ↓

← CHLOE

MacKenzie was so angry, I thought she was going to whack me over the head with her new Kate Spade hobo purse.

"I'm warning you, Maxwell!" she hissed. "If you so much as look at me the wrong way, I'll make sure everyone sees your little Queasy Cheesy video. You'll get laughed right out of this school. Even your pity-pals, Chloe, Zoey and Brandon, will be too embarrassed to be seen with you!"

"This is a talent show, MacKenzie. Did it ever occur to you to try winning by using your . . . um . . . TALENT? Or is that a problem because you don't have any?"

MacKenzie took a step towards me and put her hands on her hips. "Better yet, maybe I'll just send out a text about your big secret. That you don't belong here, and your dad—"

"WHATEVER!" I shouted. "Like I really care what people think about me at this school!"

But I do care. And just the thought of her threats made me break into a cold, clammy sweat. My throat was so tight I could hardly breathe.

"Honestly, MacKenzie! The talent show is NOT

that big of a deal to me and definitely isn't worth dealing with all your drama."

"Well, it's a big deal to ME! I DESERVE my fifteen minutes of fame, so stay out of my way."

Then MacKenzie smirked and flipped her hair in my face (like she was all that and a bag of chips) and wrinkled her perfect little nose at me.

"OMG! WHAT is that HORRIBLE smell?! I think the stench of your cheap perfume is starting to overpower my expensive designer fragrance. What did you spray on this morning, Macaroni Cheese?!"

I just gritted my teeth and rolled my eyes at her. Is it a crime to eat mac and cheese for breakfast?! We were out of cereal!! ☹!

Then MacKenzie turned and sashayed down the hall. I just HATE it when she sashays!!

I was about to open my locker when I was practically trampled alive by a large group of CCP girls.

"OMG, MacKenzie! We just heard about your dance group!"

"Everyone knows you're going to win!"

"Mac's Maniacs ROCKS! Can I join?"

"Wait up, MacKenzie! Wait up!"

They scrambled after MacKenzie like mindless . . . lip-gloss-wearing . . . zombie . . . baby ducks or something.

I just stood there staring at the front of my
locker like an IDIOT. I felt SO HUMILIATED!

Hot tears flooded my eyes and I tried my best to
blink them away.

However, instead of crying, I decided to rip
MacKenzie's flyer into a million little pieces.

At this point I want nothing WHATSOEVER to do with MacKenzie. Or that stupid talent show!

I'll be SO glad when this HORRIBLE day is over. ☹!!

I'm so sick and tired of MacKenzie manipulating me,
I could

SCREAM!

I can't believe she's trying to keep me from
competing in the talent show.

It's like she's OBSESSED with winning it. Her ego is
SO BIG it has stretch marks!

I think the best thing for me to do is avoid her like
the plague. Which is NOT going to be easy, because
my locker is right next to hers.

I've decided that mentioning the video to my parents
would just make things worse.

My mom would gush about how talented and
ADORABLE Brianna and I were and would
probably e-mail the darn thing to half a million
people.

And of course, if I told Chloe and Zoey, the FIRST thing they'd want to do is watch it.

Which would be SUPERembarrassing!!!

And if Brandon saw it . . . OMG!!

He'd realize what a hopeless LOSER I am ☹!

NOTE TO SELF: Continue to check the video daily to monitor how many times it's been viewed.

As if things weren't already a hot mess, today was the second time this week I've seen bugs inside the school building.

I counted nine huge bugs in the girls' locker room just while I was getting dressed after gym class.

One flew in my hair, and I totally

FREAKED!

Of course, MacKenzie and the CCPs were practically rolling on the floor laughing at me.

Thank goodness Chloe and Zoey were there to help me. They are the best friends EVER!

As crazy as this may sound, BUGS are the very

reason I'll NEVER, EVER fit in at this school. Mostly because I have a

DEEP, DARK SECRET!!

I only attend this fancy prep school because my dad arranged a scholarship for me as part of his BUG EXTERMINATION CONTRACT!

OMG!! I'm SO totally EMBARRASSED about it, I haven't even told Chloe and Zoey. Yet!

As a matter of fact, I've been at WCD for almost three months now, and not a single student here knows my secret.

Well, no one except . . . MACKENZIE HOLLISTER ☹! And she found out purely by accident.

One morning I was late for school and the only way I could get there was in my dad's work van. I've always been a little worried about riding with him because his van is old, needs a tune-up and has a lot of things wrong with it — the most serious being the GINORMOUS roach sitting on top of it.

People stop right in their tracks and stare at it in awe.

Not only is it hideous-looking, but it makes you feel really . . . . ODD.

Anyway, when Dad dropped me off at the front door of the school, I was superhappy and relieved that no one else was around to see me.

But then MacKenzie just unexpectedly POPPED OUT of nowhere. Like some kind of EVIL jack-in-the-box.

POP

When I saw her standing there, I almost had a heart attack!

She was like this really big, ugly, infected spot that had suddenly erupted right on the tip of the nose of . . . my LIFE!!

She stared at me with this shocked look on her face and said, "What is that hideous brown thing on top of your van . . . ?!"

I just rolled my eyes at her because, personally, I thought that was the STUPIDEST question ever.

It was OBVIOUS to anyone with a BRAIN that it was a cockroach, and it was up there on top of our van mainly to . . . um . . . do really important . . . stuff that was . . . um, actually NONE of MacKenzie's business!!

But the strange thing was that MacKenzie hadn't mentioned my dad again until yesterday.

And she's one of the biggest gossips in the entire school.

I've heard other kids gush that MacKenzie is so rich, she was born with a silver spoon in her mouth.

NOT!! MacKenzie's mouth is so big, she was born with a silver SHOVEL in it!

WAAAA!!

SILVER SPOON SHOVEL

That girl CANNOT be trusted! ☹!!

HELP!! It's only 7:30 a.m. and my day is already a

TOTAL DISASTER !!

I'm beginning to think transferring to a new school might not be such a bad idea after all.

Which, BTW, would probably make MacKenzie

SUPERHAPPY!

I got up extra early this morning to finish my geometry homework.

I was just chilling out, eating a big bowl of delicious

Fruity Pebbles cereal and daydreaming about
BRANDON . . .

MY BRANDON
DAYDREAM

ME

. . . when suddenly the telephone rang.

I had a really bad feeling about that call, even
before I answered it.

Then, when I realized who it was, I just about had a
heart attack right there on the spot!

ME →

WHAT I SAID: Hello . . .

WHAT HE SAID: Hi, this is Principal Winston. I'm calling for Maxwell's Bug Extermination. We've recently started having an insect problem at the school and I'm a little concerned.

WHAT I SAID: (GASP!) Um . . . you've reached Maxwell's Bug Extermination. We're currently away from the phone. Please leave a message at the tone and we'll return your call. Um . . . BEEEEEEP!

WHAT HE SAID: Yes, Principal Winston here, from Westchester Country Day Middle School. We need your services for a serious insect problem. Could you stop by my office tomorrow during school hours? I'll give you all the details when we meet. Thanks!

PRINCIPAL WINSTON →

Still in a daze, I hung up the phone, grabbed my lucky pen and filled out a message sheet for Dad:

FOR: __DAD__   URGENT ☒

DATE: __Thurs., Nov. 7TH__ TIME: __7:15__ (AM) PM

WHILE YOU WERE OUT

FROM: __Principal Winston__

OF: __WCD Middle School__

PHONE: __You already have it__
AREA CODE   NUMBER   EXTENSION

TELEPHONED	☒	PLEASE CALL	
CAME TO SEE YOU		WILL CALL AGAIN	
RETURNED CALL		WANTS TO SEE YOU	☒

MESSAGE: __Needs you to come to__
__WCD to discuss a bug problem.__
__Stop by his office during__
__school hours, Friday, Nov. 8th.__

SIGNED: NIKKI ☺

That's when the extreme AWFULNESS of the situation FINALLY started to sink in and

I TOTALLY LOST IT!

69

70

My principal wants my *DAD* to come to my

SCHOOL

to take care of the *BUG PROBLEM?!!*

My stomach got really icky like I had just eaten at Queasy Cheesy or something.

And I thought I was going to faint.

However, rather than waiting to DIE of embarrassment at school, I decided to take the initiative and end it all right then ☹!

By DROWNING myself ☹!

In my delicious bowl of Fruity Pebbles ☺!!!

I know it sounds like an INSANE idea. But I'd already tried it on Miss Penelope, my sister's hand puppet, and it had actually worked. Kind of.

ME, DESPERATELY TRYING TO DROWN MY SORROWS IN MY BOWL OF CEREAL!

However, in spite of my efforts, I ended up STILL very much ALIVE.

I felt so frustrated with my situation, I wanted to SCREAM! Again.

Mostly because I had loads of soggy Fruity Pebble thingies stuck up my nose.

OMG! I must have sneezed Fruity Pebbles for, like, ten minutes straight.

They were plastered all over the walls and ceiling like rainbow-coloured boogers or something.

I can't believe Principal Winston is expecting my dad to show up at his office tomorrow for a bug extermination appointment!!!

I'll TRANSFER SCHOOLS before I let my dad HUMILIATE me by DANCING around in his red jumpsuit (which, BTW, has MY last name plastered across the back), ZAPPING BUGS in front of the ENTIRE student body ☹!!

Everyone will think he forgot to take his meds or something.

I've officially designated my school as a . . .

NO-DAD ZONE!!

NO WAY AM I TELLING HIM ABOUT THAT
PHONE MESSAGE!!

It just AIN'T gonna happen!!

After Dad misses that appointment, hopefully
Principal Winston will just hire someone else to take
care of the school's bugs.

I already HAVE the scholarship.

So what is Winston going to do? Suddenly just kick
me out?! In the middle of the semester?! NOT!!

I think I'm going to wear my lucky socks tomorrow.

Hey, I'm gonna need all the help I can get.

☹!!

All day I've been a NERVOUS WRECK!

I felt superguilty about not giving my dad that telephone message.

But more than anything, I was

ABSOLUTELY TERRIFIED

I was going to see PRINCIPAL WINSTON in the halls.

I don't have anything against him personally. He's a little weird, yes. But so are MOST principals and teachers.

I mean, who wouldn't be TOTALLY INSANE after ten or fifteen years at a middle school?!!

Just hanging around this place as a STUDENT for a couple of years can be psychologically damaging ☹!

Anyway, I was afraid Winston was going to mention something to me about my dad's appointment to exterminate bugs for the school.

That's when I decided it was superimportant for me to wear a very clever and cunning disguise so Winston wouldn't recognize me.

But, unfortunately, I didn't have much to work with. Just my not-from-the-mall hoodie (with lint balls on it), a little imagination and a lot of desperation. . .

ME, IN A VERY CLEVER AND CUNNING DISGUISE

Not only was it brilliantly simple, but comfortable and FREE!

Luckily, my disguise worked just as I'd planned ☺!

When Principal Winston saw me after French class, he couldn't tell I was actually ME! And he didn't mention my dad or needing an exterminator, THANK GOODNESS ☺!

He just looked a little freaked out. Probably because I was staring at him to test my disguise.

?!

WHAT THE...?!

ME STARING

78

Then Principal Winston did the strangest thing.

He cleared his throat really loudly and told me to skip my next class and go STRAIGHT to the office to get a four-hour pass to visit the guidance counsellor!

At first I thought he was making a little joke or something.

But then I realized he ACTUALLY believed I was a seriously mentally ill WEIRDO!!

Now, how CRAZY is THAT?!

However, the good news was that I was getting out of four hours of class! SQUEEEEEEE ☺!!

Of course, I fixed my hoodie BEFORE I went to the guidance counsellor's office. I didn't want HER to mistake me for a seriously mentally ill weirdo too.

We talked about how my classes were coming along and reviewed my new class schedule for next semester.

Then, after lunch, she made me watch this superboring video series about career planning.

The four hours went by pretty quickly, and before I knew it, she handed me a pass to go back to class.

I really wanted to find Chloe and Zoey to tell them the exciting news about Principal Winston sending me to the guidance counsellor.

But the school day was pretty much over, and it was time to go home. SQUEEEEEEE ☺!!

The very best part was that Principal Winston DIDN'T mention my dad! And my dad DIDN'T show up for that appointment!

My flawless strategic planning, along with my very clever disguise, saved the day!

Am I NOT brilliant?!!

☺!!

SATURDAY, NOVEMBER 9

Today my mom came up with the stupid idea that we need to have "Family Sharing Time".

She patiently explained to us that "spending preplanned quality time together as a family would encourage love, mutual respect and bonding."

I patiently explained to HER that she should STOP watching *Dr Phil.*

Since we were stuck doing "Family Sharing Time", I suggested we try one of those cool EXTREME SPORTS they show on MTV.

You know, the kind where you get to wear a helmet with cute designs on it, like hearts or rainbows.

So you'll look really cute when you break a leg or fracture your skull.

I think it would be fun, exciting and educational if our family went BUNGEE JUMPING together ☺!

Okay, so maybe a family bungee-jumping trip is NOT such a good idea!

As expected, my parents complained that extreme sports were way too dangerous.

But that was a lame excuse, because "Family Sharing Time" can be ten times more DEADLY than all the extreme sports combined!

Like the activity they'd planned for today.

My parents excitedly announced at breakfast that we were going canoeing.

I almost choked on my waffle!

(It didn't have anything to do with the fact that we were going canoeing. I just eat really fast and tend to almost choke on my food on a regular basis.)

Anyway, my dad had purchased an old, beaten-up canoe at a garage sale for $3.00.

He had his heart set on trying it out before winter sets in and all the lakes freeze over.

I was like, "Three dollars?! Dad, are you KA-RAY-ZEE?!! You spend more than that on your Egg McMuffin meal!"

But I just said that inside my head, so no one else heard it but me.

What IDIOT would risk taking his/her family out in deep water in a garage sale canoe that ONLY cost $3.00?!!

Okay, let me rephrase the question . . .

What idiot . . . OTHER than my DAD?! I love him and all, but sometimes I REALLY worry about that guy!

Even a tiny, cheap, plastic pink canoe for Brianna's doll costs MORE than $3.00!

I'm just saying. . . !

DAD'S CANOE
$3

DOLL'S CANOE
$17

The really scary part was that Dad knew nothing
whatsoever about canoes.

And since his was from a garage sale, it didn't
come with a manual, instruction book, warranty, or
ANYTHING!

When I mentioned my concerns, Dad just rolled his eyes at me and said, "Hey! I don't need to be a rocket doctor to locate the ON/OFF switch."

Anyway, Mom made sandwiches, Dad packed the car and we headed out to this huge bay area that's really popular with boaters.

As I expected, the event quickly turned into a major DISASTER.

Mainly because Dad didn't figure out that a canoe required paddles until AFTER we got out onto the water.

And then he got an attitude about the whole thing because HIS canoe didn't come with any paddles OR an ON/OFF switch (DUH!).

Which was probably WHY it only cost $3.00.

But I didn't bother to remind Dad of all that stuff, because he was kind of in a really bad mood.

So there we were, just floating around out on the bay for what seemed like FOREVER!

Thank goodness it was an unseasonably warm day or we could have got hypothermia or something.

Suddenly Dad's face lit up, and I knew he was getting another of his WACKY ideas.

He grabbed this large stick that was floating in the water. Then he took off his shirt, tied it to the stick and let it flutter in the wind.

I guessed that he was trying to convert our paddle-less canoe into a sailboat or something.

But, like most of his ideas, it didn't quite work the way he expected.

Whenever the wind blew, the canoe would just spin around in circles really fast, like some kind of demonic amusement park ride.

Of course we were all a bit grumpy about our situation.

But thanks to Dad, now we were GRUMPY, DIZZY and SEASICK ☹!

And Mom was starting to get on my LAST nerve!

Being the eternal optimist, she tried to cheer us up by making us sing "Row, Row, Row Your Boat"!

That's when I suddenly lost it and screamed, "Mom, has your reality check bounced?! Can't you see we don't have any PADDLES? How are we supposed to ROW, ROW, ROW the boat?!"

But I just said that inside my head, so no one else heard it but me.

And Brianna would NOT shut up! I had to restrain myself from trying to strangle her.

She was whining NONSTOP about the STUPIDEST things. . .

Okay, I love my family and everything. But sometimes I think they're, um . . .

A FEW CLOWNS SHORT OF A CIRCUS!!

Luckily for us, someone spotted Dad's homemade sail and assumed he was signaling for help.

Even though our "Family Sharing Time" activity got off to a really bad start, I have to admit it ended up being as exciting as any extreme sport.

WHY? Getting rescued by that Coast Guard helicopter was thrilling.

And being transported back to our car in that sleek, superfast police speedboat was a total RUSH!

When we finally got home, I was surprised to hear a phone message from Chloe and Zoey.

"Hey, Nikki, what's up? It's Chloe and Zoey here! We're calling to see if you're going to be available today or tomorrow to work on our act for the talent show. If so, give us a call. We can't wait to get started!"

I was like, Just great ☹! I really wanted to be in

the talent show with them, but MacKenzie was going to make my life totally miserable if I did.

Sooner or later I was going to have to tell my BFFs I wouldn't be performing with them.

But I was so exhausted from our canoe trip, I just wanted to take a hot shower and crawl into my comfy bed.

I decided to tell them . . . LATER!

I wonder if Dad has figured out yet that canoes DON'T have ON/OFF switches. . . ?

Mom and I are getting ready to go shopping to buy me some new clothes. I can hardly believe it!

I guess I owe Brianna a big thankyou since she's pretty much the person responsible for it.

It all started when Mom gave Brianna a new paint set and easel. She said it would help Brianna develop her artistic abilities.

So Brianna started painting, and Mom's been plastering her artwork all over the house.

The thing that really freaked me out, though, was this large portrait she drew of ME.

I couldn't believe Mom actually taped it up on our refrigerator like that.

What if a total stranger just randomly wandered into our house and saw Brianna's drawing up there?!

Hey, it could happen!!

But mostly that portrait was very damaging to my self-esteem.

I realize I'm not supercute like the girls in the CCP clique at my school. But PUH-LEEZE! Does my face really look like it got run over by a bus?!

And as if all that wasn't bad enough, Brianna is a very messy artist. She splatters paint EVERYWHERE!

I almost died when she actually got paint on my favourite shirt.

OMG! I had a hissy fit right there on the spot.

Okay, I'll admit it. That spot of paint on my shirt WAS kind of small.

But the last time I watched Judge Judy on television, she specifically stated, "Parents are responsible for the damage their child does to the property of other people. And that's the LAW, you @#$%& IDIOT!!" Or something like that.

Everyone knows Judge Judy is a very fair and impartial judge. She's also supergrumpy and possibly a little senile!

Of course, my mom took Brianna's side like she always does. She said, "Nikki, I'm sure it was an accident. I'll replace anything she gets paint on. Okay?"

I just looked at my mom and rolled my eyes.

"Yeah, right! And what if Brianna gets paint on ALL my clothes? Then you're going to buy me a whole new wardrobe?!" But I just said that inside my head, so no one else heard it but me.

Suddenly I had the most brilliant idea. That's when I decided to inspire Brianna's creativeness by finding stuff for her to paint.

I gave her my shirt to get started on. Then I ran upstairs to my room and tossed most of my clothes into a big laundry basket.

It felt really good helping my little sister develop her artistic skills.

Mom was really shocked when she discovered that Brianna had painted almost all my clothes.

Of course, I didn't tell her the part about it all being MY idea ☺!

Mom tried her best to weasel out of her promise to replace the clothes that Brianna got paint on. But I reminded her that as an impressionable young child, I was learning the importance of honesty, integrity and keeping one's word from the example being set by my parents.

Which is the drivel I've picked up from all those TV talk shows.

Anyway, Mom felt SO guilty, she finally agreed to honour her promise.

Now I get to . . .

SHOP TILL I DROP!

SQUEEEEEEE ☺!!

BTW, I finally returned the call to both Chloe and Zoey.

I let them know that even though we weren't able to get together to practise over the weekend, we could meet to discuss our plans tomorrow in the library.

Which means I have to make a final decision tomorrow!!

What am I going to do???!!!

I'm so CONFUSED! I feel like my brain is going to EXPLODE!!

Every day during study hall, Chloe, Zoey and I are excused to go work as library shelving assistants, or LSAs. We LOVE our job!

ME, CHLOE & ZOEY WORKING REALLY
HARD PUTTING AWAY LIBRARY BOOKS
(WELL, SORT OF. . .)

After we finally got all the books reshelved, Zoey suggested that we decide what we were going to do for our talent show act.

That's when Chloe suddenly started doing what looked like the funky chicken.

CHLOE

Which meant she had just had a REALLY GREAT idea for the talent show.

"OMG! OMG! I just got the most FABULOUS idea! We can do a wicked cool dance routine about books. We'll call ourselves the BREAK-DANCING BOOKWORMS!" Chloe gushed.

"I LOVE IT! I LOVE IT!" Zoey squealed. "We can make fuzzy lime green costumes that look like caterpillars. And we can rap too! What do you think, Nikki?"

I was like, "Actually, Chloe and Zoey, it sounds like a really fun idea. But is this supposed to be a TALENT show or a FREAK show?!"

But I just said that inside my head, so no one else heard it but me.

Chloe and Zoey are the BEST friends EVER! But they're also the second- and third-biggest dorks in the entire school.

So sometimes their ideas are a little . . . how should I say it . . . DORKY too.

CHLOE & ZOEY'S WACKY IDEA #1,397:
BREAK-DANCING BOOKWORMS

But their occasionally weird antics are the reason they are so much fun to hang out with.

I took a deep breath and tried my best to break it to them gently.

"Actually, I think it's a really cute idea. But I have a

bit of bad news. As much as I was looking forward to it, I've decided not to participate in the talent show this year. I'm trying to . . . um, spend more time on, um . . . schoolwork and stuff."

"Nikki! It's not going to be fun unless all three of us do this together!" Chloe groaned as her smile quickly faded.

Zoey looked disappointed too. "Well, if YOU'RE not going to be in the talent show, then I don't want to be in it!"

"Me neither!" Chloe said grimly.

"Come on, guys! You can be break-dancing bookworms TOGETHER. It'll STILL be fun!" I said, trying to sound upbeat.

But I couldn't get them to change their minds.

The three of us just sat there not saying anything for what seemed like FOREVER.

To make matters worse, I was starting to feel guilty about letting them down.

Finally Zoey broke the silence. "Nikki, are you mad at us or something?"

"WHAT are you talking about? Of course not!" I answered. "If anything, you two should be mad at me!"

"You've been kind of quiet lately. Is anything wrong?" Chloe asked, staring at me intently.

For a split second I thought about just pouring my heart out to them both.

About MacKenzie, Queasy Cheesy, the talent show, my dad, my scholarship . . .

EVERYTHING!

But instead, I shook my head vigorously and tried to muster a big smile.

"NO! Nothing's wrong! I just feel terrible that you guys have decided not to be in the talent show. I know you were really looking forward to it."

Chloe shrugged and looked out the window.

Zoey bit her lip and stared at the floor.

I reminded myself I was doing all this for their own good. The last thing I wanted was for THEM to be a casualty in MacKenzie's war against ME.

Finally the bell rang, ending the school day.

Chloe and Zoey looked sad and flustered. I think they knew I was hiding something.

And I felt just . . . AWFUL!

I sighed and tried to apologize. "Listen, I'm REALLY, REALLY sorry, okay?"

As Chloe and Zoey got up to leave, they both sadly muttered the exact same thing at the exact same time.

WHATEVER.

Then they turned and walked away ☹.

I think I've finally figured out the source of the bug problem at our school!

I'm no expert (unlike my dad!), but it was kind of strange to see so many different bugs just randomly crawling around like that.

But here's the crazy part!

I accidentally left my French homework in my locker and my teacher let me leave class to go get it. While I was at my locker, the halls were empty and totally quiet.

I could have sworn I heard CRICKETS CHIRPING!

And the sound was coming from
MACKENZIE'S LOCKER!!!

I was like, What the. . .!!

I stood on my tippy toes and tried to peek through

the slot thingy at the top of MacKenzie's locker.

I thought I saw the silver lid of a jar or something, but her big leather bag was in the way.

That's when I got the brilliant idea to stick my ruler through the slot thingy to move stuff around and get a better look inside.

After a few tries I was able to push MacKenzie's bag out of the way.

And sure enough, right behind it was a glass jar. But I couldn't quite see if anything was inside it.

Using the ruler, I tried to scoot the jar towards the front so I could get a closer look.

But I somehow accidentally knocked it over, and it hit the locker door with a *KLUNK* and rolled on top of the bag.

That's when I noticed that the lid must not have been on very tight or something because it flipped right off.

I was like, OOPSIE! Time to get back to class!

But the longer I stood there thinking about it, the ANGRIER I got.

Mainly because it looked to me like MacKenzie had been secretly planting bugs all over the school.

She KNEW that sooner or later the school was going to call my dad to exterminate the place. And when it did, I was going to have a complete MELTDOWN.

There was NO WAY I was letting my dad come to my school.

I mean, what if he saw ME in the hallway between classes?!!

He might say something SUPERembarrassing to me like, "Hi there, Nikki. . . !"

Then, OMG!! I'd just keel over and . . . DIE!!!

And from that day forward, I'd be known as the daughter of that crazy disco-dancing exterminator.

Kids would whisper stuff about me behind my back and call me a FREAK!

And not just a regular FREAK, but a half-BUG, half-DORK FREAK! Which is, like, ten times WORSE!!!

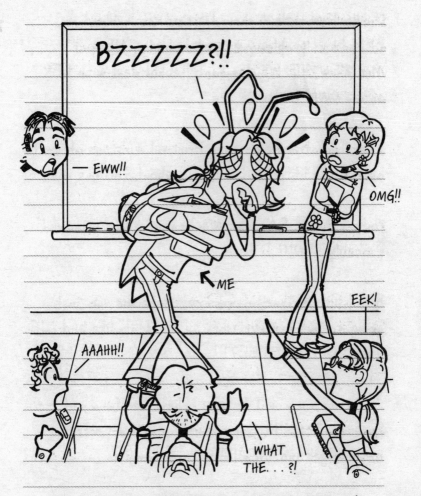

ME, THE HALF-BUG, HALF-DORK FREAK!

My life would be TOTALLY RUINED!! And it would all be MACKENZIE'S FAULT ☹!!

Unlike that talent show fiasco that involved my BFFs, this problem was just between ME and MACKENZIE. Which meant I could deal with HER on my OWN terms.

I marched straight down to Principal Winston's office to have a nice little chat with him about this bug issue.

Only, I didn't RAT out MacKenzie! YES, I know! I probably SHOULD have.

But I already knew from experience she was just going to bat her eyelashes all innocent-like and LIE THROUGH HER TEETH!

And Winston would totally believe her (and not me) because all adults think MacKenzie is a perfect little angel and INCAPABLE of lying.

Besides, I was going to talk to Winston about something WAY more important than MacKenzie's juvenile little pranks.

Our meeting went just as I had planned.

He told me he was happy I'd stopped by his office and asked how things were going as a new student.

I took a deep breath and got right to the point.

"Actually, Principal Winston, I'm doing fine considering the fact that I'm stuck with a locker right next to MacKenzie Hollister, and I'm totally lost in geometry. But I stopped by to let you know that since my dad is superbusy right now, you should just call in another exterminator. I'm really sure he appreciates your business and all, but there's only so much work he can handle."

Principal Winston blinked. Then he took off his glasses, folded his arms across his chest and slowly nodded.

"Is that so? I was wondering why your dad missed our appointment on Friday. I thought maybe he didn't get the message I left on your answering machine. Well, it's quite a coincidence that you dropped by, Miss Maxwell, because I was planning to give him another call this afternoon."

"Well, if you want some advice, don't bother! He's so busy he hasn't even . . . slept in like, um . . . three or five days. Plus, it would be healthier for his . . . you know . . . sick gallbladder and stuff, if you just got someone else."

Principal Winston sat there staring at me with this really perplexed look on his face. Then I saw him glance at the telephone on his desk.

That's when I stood up, plastered a fake smile on my face and shook his hand real friendlylike.

"Well, Principal Winston, I don't want to take up any more of your time. I know you're a busy man. Plus, I just heard the bell for lunch and I LOVE all the creative things your cooks do with mystery meat. I'm really, really glad we had this little chat."

"Thank you, Miss Maxwell. I'm glad we did too," he said, and cleared his throat.

Then I got the heck outta there!

As I headed down the hall towards the cafeteria, I felt like a huge burden had been lifted off my shoulders.

Winston was going to use another exterminator and my secret would be safe again.

Problem solved!

As I got to the door of the cafeteria, a dozen CCP girls rushed past me screaming.

Inside, it was total

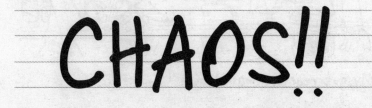

I immediately spotted MacKenzie standing on top of a lunch table shrieking hysterically and pointing at something lying on the floor in front of the salad bar.

My gut reaction was: Mouse?! Snake?!

But seeing as it was MacKenzie, it also could have been something as mundanely horrifying as a pair of red polyester trousers. I have to admit, I wasn't all that surprised to see . . .

MACKENZIE'S BIG LEATHER BAG!!

That's when I finally came to the conclusion that my earlier hunch was correct.

I guess there really WERE crickets in that jar! ☺!!

WEDNESDAY, NOVEMBER 13

The only thing everyone is talking about these days is that stupid talent show.

And it's really starting to get on my nerves!

People are practising before school, after school and even during lunch.

I'll be SO happy when all this is over!

I'd been waiting for MacKenzie to ask Chloe and Zoey to join her dance squad, so I wasn't surprised when she approached them about it after gym class today.

However, I was shocked when Chloe and Zoey turned her down!

They actually told her they didn't want to be in the talent show unless I was in it too. I couldn't believe my BFFs had basically told MacKenzie to take her little dance group and flush it ☺!!

MacKenzie just stared at them with her mouth hanging open because she suddenly realized her plan to keep me out of the talent show had backfired.

She must have seen the smirk on my face because she gave me this really dirty look, and I was like, "WHAT?!" and batted my eyes all innocentlike.

I could NOT believe the disgusting, low-down, dirty thing MacKenzie did next.

"Okay, Chloe and Zoey. I'll be honest with you. Jason and Ryan have been BEGGING me to ask you to join. They're DYING to be your dance partners. I promised I wouldn't tell, but those guys have really big crushes on you two!" she gushed, and then winked.

There was no doubt in my mind that MacKenzie was lying like a rug. She was only pretending to be Miss Matchmaker to trick Chloe and Zoey into joining.

But they believed every word she said and totally lost it. They started jumping up and down and squealing!

I didn't have the heart to tell them MacKenzie was a pathological liar and Jason and Ryan were probably in on her little scheme.

I shot MacKenzie a dirty look, and this time SHE batted her eyes at ME all innocent-like and said, "WHAT?!"

I was so mad I could SPIT! I wanted to slap that girl into tomorrow for playing with my friends' emotions like that.

Those two guys had taken cheerleaders to the Halloween dance two weeks ago and practically broken Chloe's and Zoey's hearts.

And NOW they were all going to be dance partners?!! I couldn't believe MacKenzie was such a little MANIPULATIVE . . . beady-eyed . . . SNAKE!!

What REALLY worried me, though, was the fact that neither Chloe nor Zoey had fully recovered from their totally debilitating case of . . .

CRUSH-ITIS ☹!!

DR NIKKI SHARES SOME GOOD NEWS!

"Well, girls! From your test results, it appears your severe case of crush—itis can be cured with medication."

DR NIKKI SHARES SOME NOT-SO-GOOD NEWS!

"Unfortunately, you won't be able to sit down for a week. Now roll over, close your eyes and count to ten."

MacKenzie was recklessly exposing Chloe and Zoey to yet another dangerous case of CRUSH-ITIS, merely for selfish gain. That girl is HEARTLESS!

So now they start dance practice tomorrow.

I probably won't be seeing much of my BFFs over the next two weeks because they'll be hanging out with MacKenzie and the CCPs.

But it's not like I'm jealous or anything.

I mean, how juvenile would THAT be?!

☹!!

OMG!!

I can't believe the

HORRIBLE

mess I've made!

I had no idea things were going to turn out like this.

WHAT am I going to do now?!

I think I'm going to be

SICK!

Which is the reason I asked my geometry teacher, Mrs Sprague, if I could be excused to go to the bathroom.

ME

ME, IN THE BATHROOM FEELING VERY
WORRIED & SICK!!

Okay, this is what happened. . .

When I got home from school yesterday, I stopped
to get the mail.

I saw an envelope from WCD that was addressed to both me and my parents and figured it was my report card or something.

However, when I opened it, I had a heart attack right there on the spot because it was a TUITION BILL ☹!!

How did I know?

Mainly because it said in really big letters:

NIKKI MAXWELL TUITION BILL.

And below that was a dollar amount so big, I almost thought my eyeballs were going to rupture just looking at it.

I could try to pay it off with my teeny allowance. But that would take 1,829.7 years ☹!

ME, TRYING TO READ MY TUITION BILL WITH
MY ALMOST RUPTURED EYEBALLS!

At first I thought it was some kind of mistake!!

But the only logical explanation is that I had messed
up big time by NOT giving my dad that phone
message from Principal Winston.

Then I had very STUPIDLY gone to Winston's office

and told him my dad was too busy to come in. And now my scholarship has been revoked!!

WHAT was I thinking?!!! There's just no way my parents can afford to pay that tuition bill!

Suddenly it became very clear that MacKenzie had completely set me up!

Her master plan WASN'T to embarrass me by having my dad come to the school to exterminate all the bugs she was letting loose.

NUH-UH!! Her little brain was way more DEVIOUS than that!

Her plan was for my dad NOT to come to the school to exterminate all the bugs she was letting loose.

So I'd lose my SCHOLARSHIP and GET KICKED OUT OF SCHOOL!

She knew I'd be FRANTIC and do everything within my power to keep him away.

Basically, she TRICKED me into RUINING MY OWN LIFE 😞!!

MacKenzie Hollister is an

EVIL GENIUS!

I had no scholarship and I had no money to pay the tuition.

My situation was **HOPELESS!**

As I sat there on that cold bathroom floor a thick cloud of anguish seemed to descend upon my stall like some kind of putrid smog, making it nearly impossible for me to breathe or think clearly.

Overcome by gut-wrenching emotion (and overwhelmed by that awful school bathroom smell), I began to ponder the unthinkable.

I wanted all my problems to go away.

So I decided to just end it all right there, by . . .

FLUSHING MYSELF DOWN THE TOILET ☹!!

But, unfortunately, I was WAY too big to fit down that little drain-hole thingy.

That's when I noticed a bright yellow talent show poster taped on the stall door.

I'd seen them plastered around the school for days. But after all the drama with MacKenzie, I had never bothered to actually read one. . .

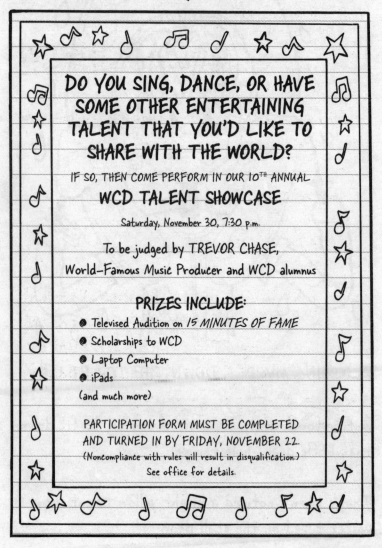

DO YOU SING, DANCE, OR HAVE SOME OTHER ENTERTAINING TALENT THAT YOU'D LIKE TO SHARE WITH THE WORLD?

IF SO, THEN COME PERFORM IN OUR 10TH ANNUAL

WCD TALENT SHOWCASE

Saturday, November 30, 7:30 p.m.

To be judged by TREVOR CHASE,
World-Famous Music Producer and WCD alumnus

PRIZES INCLUDE:

● Televised Audition on *15 MINUTES OF FAME*
● Scholarships to WCD
● Laptop Computer
● iPads

(and much more)

PARTICIPATION FORM MUST BE COMPLETED AND TURNED IN BY FRIDAY, NOVEMBER 22.
(Noncompliance with rules will result in disqualification.)
See office for details.

I had to read that poster, like, three times before it finally sank in.

WCD was actually giving away

FULL SCHOLARSHIPS?!

I know I swore off the talent show earlier, but now things have changed.

I'm desperate.

How desperate am I?!

REALLY, REALLY, REALLY, REALLY, REALLY, REALLY, REALLY, REALLY, REALLY, REALLY, REALLY, REALLY, REALLY, REALLY, REALLY, REALLY, REALLY, REALLY, REALLY, REALLY

DESPERATE!!

☹!!

Just when I thought my life COULDN'T get any WORSE, IT DID!!

I skipped lunch today because I wanted to talk to Brandon.

I really felt the need to vent to someone about all the stuff that was going wrong in my life right now, like for example . . .

EVERYTHING ☹!!!

Confiding in Chloe and Zoey was not an option since they were busy rehearsing with Jason and Ryan during lunch.

I still considered Brandon a good friend even though he's been so busy that we've barely spoken to each other since the dance two weeks ago.

It always seemed like talking to him helped me think things through more logically.

But most important, I wanted to tell him about my dad, my revoked scholarship and that I might be leaving WCD very soon.

I'm just really tired of pretending everything is fine when it isn't!

And I know at some point MacKenzie is going to blab all my business to the entire school anyway.

Hey, world! My dad is a bug exterminator and I attend WCD on a scholarship!

Big deal! It's WHO I really am!

WHY should I be ashamed of it?!

Even if MacKenzie has a problem with it, I don't have to.

Anyway, I rushed down to the newspaper office, since that's where Brandon has been hanging out lately training some new photographer.

Well, it looks like he's been pretty busy, all right. . .

WITH MACKENZIE!!

I've always wondered if Brandon really likes me or not. Well, now I know.

HE DOESN'T!!!

I think he's just been using me all along to make MacKenzie jealous or something.

I couldn't stand to watch her gushing all over him like a lovesick puppy.

"Oh, Braaaandon!" this and "Oh, Braaaaandon!" that.

OMG! She sounded so DITZY, I thought her brains were going to ooze out of her ears like syrup and make a puddle right on the floor.

She's more CRAZY about him than EVER!

And since WHEN has MacKenzie been into photography?!!

Probably since landing BRANDON as her NEW TUTOR!

And get this! She doesn't even READ our school newspaper, because she says it doesn't have a Fashion & Style section. And the Fashion & Style section is the ONLY thing she says is worth reading in ANY newspaper.

The girl is DESPERATE!!

Anyway, I just turned around and walked right out of the room before they even saw me.

If Brandon wants MacKenzie, he can have her!!!

SATURDAY, NOVEMBER 16

My life is so MESSED UP!

All day I've been feeling SUPERdepressed and guilty.

I finally made the decision to come clean to my parents and tell them EVERYTHING!!

So what if I get grounded until my twenty-first birthday?

I was like, "Um, Mom and Dad, can I talk to you guys? It's really important!"

Mom was like, "Sure, honey. But can it wait a little bit? It's such a beautiful, clear night outside that your dad and I decided we'd all have a little Family Sharing Time."

I was like, OH, CRUD!! It was really BAD timing for "Family Sharing Time" ☹!!

Then Dad just about knocked me over rushing out

the back door with a big can of lighter fluid and a box of matches.

Is it me, or do most fathers seem to have latent pyromaniac tendencies?

They get really happy and excited whenever they grill food, light the fireplace, make a campfire, burn leaves, or do anything that involves fire. . .

DAD, WHEN SOMEONE ELSE IS IN CHARGE OF
LIGHTING THE FIRE

DAD, WHEN **HE** IS IN CHARGE OF LIGHTING THE FIRE

What's up with THAT?!

Well, tonight Dad decided to build a campfire in the backyard so we could roast marshmallows. And Mom brought out a big plate of chocolate bars and a box of crackers so we could make yummy S'MORES.

I have to admit, I was actually looking forward

to snarfing down that hot, gooey, chocolaty treat.

Sounds like a fun, family-friendly activity. Right?! It was.

Until Dad got a little carried away and burned his marshmallows to a crisp.

When they caught on fire, he totally panicked.

It looked like he was holding one of those flaming shish kebab thingies you see in fancy restaurants.

He was frantically whipping the stick around in circles trying to put out the fire.

The next thing we knew, those marshmallows were flying right off the end of his stick and practically going into orbit.

OMG! Dad's marshmallows lit up the night sky like a meteor shower or something. Actually, it looked kind of cool!

MY FAMILY, ROASTING MARSHMALLOWS

But somehow, in all the commotion, one of the flaming marshmallows landed on the front of his trouser leg and stuck there. Of course Brianna totally lost it and started screaming her head off!

Thinking fast, Mom grabbed the bucket of water Dad had placed nearby and quickly doused the front of his trousers just as they caught on fire. Thank goodness he wasn't hurt or anything.

But then our very nosy neighbour lady, Mrs Wallabanger, came running outside to see what was going on.

Dad tried his best to explain to her that while he was out in the backyard roasting marshmallows, he'd had an unfortunate little accident.

Mrs Wallabanger just stared at him with this really disgusted look on her face.

She gave Dad a lecture about how he should be ashamed of himself and actually threatened to call the police.

Then she stormed back into her house and slammed her door. But we could see her peeking out at us through her curtains.

We were all superconfused about why Mrs Wallabanger was behaving so strangely.

Until I took a closer look at Dad and realized it actually looked like he had, um . . . wet himself.

Which also pretty much explained why Mrs Wallabanger had TOTALLY FREAKED when Dad told her he'd had an "unfortunate little accident" in the backyard.

We finally decided to call it a night, and Dad put out our campfire by shovelling dirt on it.

Since Dad's trousers were wet, dirty, marshmallow-covered and slightly charred from the night's activities, Mom insisted that he take them off in the garage and throw them in the rubbish so he wouldn't make a mess in the house.

Then she rushed upstairs to get him a clean pair to put on.

Well, Mrs Wallabanger must have STILL been pretty upset, because when Mom got back to the garage to give Dad his trousers, we heard this loud commotion out in our driveway.

From what I could tell, Dad was having a really
heated argument with someone.

It sounded like a lady was trying to convince him she
was there to help him. But Dad kept insisting in a
really loud voice that he didn't WANT or NEED any
of her HELP.

That's when the lady said, "Actually, sir, I think you
need to let me HELP you FIND YOUR TROUSERS!"

← DAD

OMG! I was shocked to see that police officer! But I had to admit, she had a really good point about the trousers issue.

Then Dad got an attitude about the whole thing and told the police lady that he didn't appreciate her making a joke at his expense.

But the police lady told Dad that he needed to calm down and have a seat in the back of her squad car so they could go for a little ride down to the station.

I thought for sure Dad was going to get arrested or something.

Thank goodness Mom rushed outside and explained everything about that flaming marshmallow, the bucket of water, and Dad's no-trousers situation.

And after the nice officer lady was convinced Dad WASN'T wandering around the neighborhood peeping in neighbours' windows, she apologized to him and left.

In spite of the fact that the evening was a total

disaster, Mom still insisted that we take a picture
to put in her "Family Sharing Time" scrapbook.

So we all posed in the kitchen holding a cracker
with fake smiles plastered on our faces,
just to make her happy.

"OUR FAMILY MARSHMALLOW ROAST"
(DURING WHICH, DAD'S TROUSERS CAUGHT FIRE
AND HE NEARLY GOT ARRESTED)

This was the WORST "Family Sharing Time" ever!

Since we were all pretty traumatized from the marshmallow roast and Dad was still FURIOUS at that cop, I decided it was a VERY bad time to bring up the whole tuition bill issue.

Maybe I'll tell them tomorrow. Or I could always run away and join the circus. . . ☹!!

I was awake most of the night, tossing and turning and trying to figure out what to do about all my problems.

When I first started at WCD, I never thought in a million years I'd ever actually want to stay at this school.

But over the last couple months I guess the place has just sort of grown on me or something.

Chloe, Zoey and I have become really good friends. I actually WON the avant-garde art competition. And then Brandon asked me to the Halloween dance. Although, thanks to MacKenzie, things aren't as good as they once were ☹.

All I really need to do is figure out how to fix it all.

At this point I basically have TWO choices:

1. Just give up and transfer to a new school. . . Which means I'll ALSO have to go through the TORTURE of being the NEW KID all over again ☹!

2. Rob a bank and pay my tuition with the cash. Which, unfortunately, could be the first step in my new life as a ruthless felon.

ME, AS A RUTHLESS CRIMINAL

Instead of spending four years in high school and four years at a major university, I'll spend eight years in prison for robbery.

And when I get married and have a baby, my poor daughter will take after ME and become a juvenile delinquent while she's still in nappies.

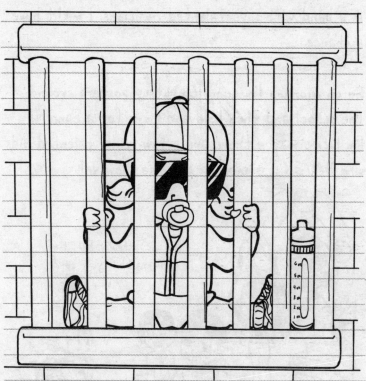

And then, while I'm rotting in prison (and having superfun mani/pedi cell-block parties with those celebs), I'll realize what a horrible mess I've made of my life and totally regret that I DIDN'T give my dad that telephone message from Principal Winston!

Anyway, the ONLY choice I really have is to try to get a scholarship by winning that talent show.

Unfortunately, I'm just an okay singer. But if I was in a band with supertalented musicians, I might have a chance.

So on Monday I'm going to put up posters around the school and then hold auditions for a band. If I'm lucky, maybe there are a few really talented kids who HAVEN'T signed up for the show yet.

Um . . . actually, BOTH of us wanna be in your band!

I arrived at school an hour early today to put up audition posters for my band.

I also got permission from the office to use the band room after school tomorrow.

I know this is last minute. But all I really need is for three or four people to show up.

Although it was still fairly early in the morning, at least a half dozen groups were already practising in various locations throughout the school.

The CCPs in the cafeteria were blasting their music so loudly I could barely hear myself think.

I peeked in and saw Chloe and Zoey dancing and flirting with Jason and Ryan. My BFFs looked SO happy.

There was no doubt in my mind that they'd enjoy dancing with Jason and Ryan more than being in my ragtag band.

I planned to tell them in the library today that I'd changed my mind about being in the talent show. I was sure they'd understand.

ME, HANGING UP MY AUDITION POSTERS

As soon as I finished hanging my posters, I rushed to class early to try to finish up some homework that I hadn't been able to complete over the weekend.

I can't believe how much homework they give you in middle school. There's just NO WAY you can get all of it done.

The last thing I needed was an incomplete, so I decided to come up with a really good excuse so my teacher would give me extra time to finish my assignment.

For some reason, teachers tend to believe stories that are really supercreative, no matter how crazy or far-fetched.

That's when I came up with the brilliant idea for a handy-dandy manual called:

THE STUDENT HANDBOOOK OF HOMEWORK EXCUSES FOR LAZY DUMMIES

I don't think there's anything like this on the market.

So I decided to write down all the best excuses I've used over the years and place them in a simple form.

And, once I've collected enough of them, I plan to

publish them as a book that could possibly become an overnight bestseller for students around the world:

FROM: _____
(YOUR NAME)

RE: Issue with My School Assignment

Dear _____,
(NAME OF TEACHER)

You probably won't believe this, but
☐ my spoiled sister
☐ my bratty brother
☐ my paranoid uncle
☐ my senile neighbour lady

has a pet
☐ snake, named Hubert,
☐ monkey, named Rocky,
☐ vampire bat, named Jean-Claude,
☐ unicorn, named Buttercup,

that unfortunately got really

- ☐ frightened
- ☐ angry
- ☐ confused
- ☐ sick

and unexpectedly

- ☐ projectile vomited on
- ☐ had babies on
- ☐ had a heart attack and died on
- ☐ had a really bad nosebleed on

my

- ☐ maths problems.
- ☐ assignment.
- ☐ project.
- ☐ report.
- ☐ homework.
- ☐ _____.

  (FILL IN THE BLANK)

When I realized I would not be turning this in to you on time, I became gravely depressed and suffered uncontrollable

- ☑ sobbing.
- ☐ flatulence.
- ☐ hiccups.
- ☐ laughter.

I am truly very sorry for any inconvenience this may have caused.

I assure you, it will *NOT* happen again

- ☐ *EVER!*
- ☐ until my next homework assignment is due.
- ☐ until the cow jumps over the moon.
- ☐ until the next exciting episode of *America's Next Top Model.*
- ☐ (and if you believe this, I'd like to sell you some ~~swamp~~ land in Florida).

Sincerely, _____
(YOUR SIGNATURE)

Hey! Maybe I can use the money from this book to pay my tuition ☺!

So, today in biology, Brandon was staring at me.

It wasn't like I was staring at HIM the entire hour or anything. I'm just very observant and happened to notice it.

I almost fell out of my chair when he leaned over and whispered, "Are you okay, Nikki? You look kind of down today."

But since talking to him would make me feel even MORE heartbroken than I already was, I just nodded and kept right on working on our human brain assignment.

Unlike MacKenzie! That girl would NOT shut up the entire hour!

OMG!

She babbled nonstop to Brandon about her new lip gloss flavours and Mac's Maniacs, all while making goo-goo eyes at him.

While observing MacKenzie's behaviour, I prepared a lab report supporting my new hypothesis on intelligence and nutrition:

It IS actually humanly possible to have the IQ of a toaster pastry and still function in society!

MACKENZIE   TOASTER PASTRY

Anyway, after class was over, Brandon didn't try to talk to me again or anything.

He just looked at me, shrugged and walked away with this perplexed look on his face.

It's almost like he has no idea WHATSOEVER why I'm acting the way I am.

Which is ironic because HE is the reason I'm a total PSYCHO.

How can he NOT know how I feel?!

But . . . what if he DOESN'T?!

What if he thinks I'm just being mean for no reason?

When I actually like him! A LOT!!

I think!

WHY am I so CONFUSED?!

☹!!

TUESDAY, NOVEMBER 19

Today was the BIG DAY! AUDITIONS!!

Although I felt superexcited, deep down I was really worried.

If I don't win the talent competition and snag a scholarship, I won't have any choice but to transfer to a new school.

Just thinking about it makes me break out in a cold sweat ☹!

And, as if I wasn't already STRESSED OUT enough, MacKenzie kept staring at me and giving me the evil eye the entire time I was at my locker.

I was like, "Hey, girlfriend. You're creeping me out. Just take a picture, why don't cha?"

But I just said that inside my head, so no one else heard it but me.

All my classes bored me out of my skull, and the day seemed to drag on and on and on.

When school was FINALLY over, I hurried towards the band room to get ready for the auditions.

As I passed the cafeteria, I couldn't help but notice MacKenzie and a few of her CCP dancers crowded around one of my audition flyers.

Of course when she saw me, she started whispering about me and giggling like an evil little witch.

ME

She had a lot of nerve to be talking about me right to my face like that.

However, since I had somewhere to be, I just ignored her and rushed right past.

I got to the band room about ten minutes early and was relieved to see a dozen or so kids warming up on their instruments.

I started to feel a lot better. But mostly I was hopeful that maybe my crazy plan was actually going to work.

I could tell they were pretty good musicians just by listening to them.

At 3:45 sharp I decided to get the show on the road.

"Okay, I'm ready to get started now, if you guys are!" I said cheerfully. "Here's the sign-up sheet."

This kinda cute guy who was drumming on the seat

of a chair looked up at me and smiled. "So, you're the one who's using the band room today? We'll be out of your hair in a minute. As soon as our tuba player shows up, we'll be moving to the choir room to practise with the glee club."

Out of my hair?! Now I was totally confused. I was pretty sure I must have heard him wrong. "Excuse me? Aren't you guys here for the talent show?"

"Yeah! We're the jazz band, and we're doing a few numbers with the glee club."

I just stared at him with my mouth dangling open. "Umm, okay. I just thought that . . . um . . . you all were here for . . ." My voice trailed off.

A guy rushed in and grabbed the tuba. Then everyone filed out of the room.

My heart sank. I groaned and collapsed into a chair.

Other than me, the room was now totally empty.

I glanced at the clock. It was 3:55.

Don't panic! I thought. *Maybe everyone is just late or something.*

I looked back at the clock and wondered if it had stopped working. It was moving so slooooooooowly.

3:58. 4:00. 4:03.

And still no one arrived.

4:05. 4:08. 4:11.

By 4:15 I sighed deeply and finally admitted the obvious.

My brilliant plan was a complete and humongous

FLOP!

NOT a single person had bothered to show up for my auditions ☹!

I couldn't remember the last time I'd felt so alone.

I got a huge lump in my throat and tried to fight back my tears.

I was such a LOSER!

Maybe transferring to another school wasn't such a bad idea after all.

It seemed VERY obvious that no one here actually liked me. I'd just been kidding myself to think so.

My thoughts were interrupted by Violet, who stormed into the room and slammed the door.

"Oh, there you are! What the HECK is going on? I told everyone they should have checked in here first! Some people are such IDIOTS!"

You ALWAYS know exactly how Violet feels about something.

Mainly because she'll tell you rather loudly whether you want to hear it or not. But I kind of like that about her.

"Well, thanks a lot for cancelling your auditions at the last minute. I've been practising that stupid song on the piano for hours! I guess fame eludes me yet again," she huffed, scowling at me.

I just shrugged and tried to wipe away my tears before she noticed them. "I'm really sorry. . ."

Suddenly her face softened, and she looked concerned. "Hey! Are you okay?"

"Sure. Just, um . . . severe . . . allergies. Actually, I'm fine. But did you just say 'cancelling'?!"

"Yeah! You did it on such short notice. What happened?"

"What do you mean, what happened?!"

"What do *YOU* mean, what do *I* mean?!" Violet looked at me like I was crazy. "You cancelled it! Right? Okay, come look at this."

I followed Violet down the hall, and we stopped at the exact spot I'd seen MacKenzie and her friends almost an hour earlier.

Violet pointed at my flyer. "SEE? It says 'CANCELLED'!"

Sure enough, scrawled across my audition flyer in black marker was the word "CANCELLED!!"

I could NOT believe my eyes!

I rushed further down the hall, to the flyer I'd posted over the drinking fountain.

It said "CANCELLED!!"

I checked the flyer on the wall near my locker.

"CANCELLED!!"

I went around the entire school ripping my "CANCELLED!!" flyers off the walls.

Then I threw them all in the rubbish.

No wonder no one had bothered to show up for my auditions.

And I knew just who was behind it all.

MACKENZIE!!!

I could feel the tears coming again. Only this time they were tears of anger.

Since it was almost time for my mom to pick me up, I decided to take a shortcut through the cafeteria to get to my locker.

My mind was racing. I still had that tuition bill and no way of paying it.

What was I going to do now? Tell my parents? It looked like that was the ONLY answer.

As I entered the cafeteria, I suddenly heard music and familiar laughter.

I froze and gasped.

JUST GREAT ☹!!

I had stumbled into MacKenzie's dance rehearsal. After what that girl had done to me, she was the LAST person I wanted to see.

I quickly slipped between two vending machines and prayed no one had spotted me. And from there I watched them practise.

I had to admit, MacKenzie and her group were really good. Especially Chloe and Zoey. As I had predicted, they were the best dancers by far.

That's when I realized my situation was hopeless. There was NO WAY I could win against her group.

As the song ended MacKenzie smiled at her dancers like a proud mother hen.

"Okay, everyone! That was FABULOUS! Let's take a ten-minute break."

Before I knew what was happening, the entire room came rushing in my direction.

Talk about CRAPPY luck!

There I was, trapped in a room with a bunch of hot, thirsty dancers.

And WHERE was I hiding? With the ice-cold sodas, juices and bottled water, of course.

I was like, Way to go, Nikki!! My stupidity never ceases to amaze me!

I turned and tried to make a dash for the door. Only I forgot about TWO little things.

Well, actually . . . TWO very BIG things. . . .

THE RUBBISH BINS!

WHAT THE . . . ?! OOPS!!

I accidentally BUMPED into the first one and then TRIPPED and FELL over the second one.

And YES! Unfortunately for me, the bins were still filled to the brim with very nasty, slimy stuff that students had either refused to eat for lunch or tossed.

And it smelled really, really . . . BAD!

Like slightly ROTTING . . . I don't even KNOW!

I hit the floor with a *THUD* and lay there stunned, covered from head to foot with disgusting rubbish.

I felt like such a KLUTZ.

I didn't know which was more painfully bruised, my BUTT or my EGO.

But the worst part was that I had an audience.

Namely, EVERY CCP in the entire school! And of course, MacKenzie was in rare form.

"OMG, Nikki! WHAT are you doing in that rubbish?! Scavenging for DINNER?"

Everyone was laughing so hard, they could barely breathe.

Well, everyone EXCEPT Chloe and Zoey.

"NIKKI! What happened?" Chloe gasped.

"OMG! Are you okay?!" Zoey asked frantically.

My two best friends each grabbed an arm and helped me to my feet. They were being SO sweet and kind to me, it almost made me cry!

MacKenzie reached into her pocket, unfolded a piece of paper, and waved it in front of my face tauntingly. It was one of my audition flyers.

"Sooo, how did your little auditions for the talent show go?! I see you chickened out and CANCELLED it at the last minute," she said.

I couldn't believe she actually said that to me. I just stood there glaring at her as I pondered which was the fouler piece of rubbish, MacKenzie or the reeking banana peel that was sliding down my forehead.

I was about to answer when both Chloe and Zoey

turned and stared at me with surprised looks on their faces.

"Wait a minute. YOU'RE going to be in the talent show?!" Chloe asked, obviously shocked.

"I thought you said you didn't have time because of your classes and homework load?!" Zoey added. "Or is it that you just didn't want to be in the talent show with US?"

"OBVIOUSLY!" MacKenzie hissed, and handed them my audition flyer. "Looks to me like she'd rather hang out with whoever wandered into her auditions than you two."

Chloe and Zoey looked very hurt.

I tried desperately to think up something to say to my BFFs.

"Actually, I, um . . . decided at the last minute and. . ."

MacKenzie quickly sized up the situation and went in for the KILL.

"Well, Chloe and Zoey, now you know what kind of BFF you have. As in, Best Fake Friend. Nikki OBVIOUSLY wanted nothing to do with you two. She doesn't deserve your friendship."

If there was an Academy Award for Best Actress in a BFF Breakup Scene, MacKenzie would have won.

"OMG! I feel so SORRY for you two . . . !" She sniffed and blinked away phony tears. Then she hugged them both like their puppy had just died.

"Chloe! Zoey! Please, please don't believe MacKenzie. I really wanted to be in the talent show with you guys. But a lot of stuff happened."

I couldn't believe how upset they were. They looked like they were going to cry.

". . . I was going to tell you about the band too. I just hadn't had the chance . . . yet!" I muttered.

"I've heard enough! Nikki is treating you like dirt. Come on, girls. We have a talent show to win!" MacKenzie grabbed Chloe and Zoey by their shoulders and led them away.

But before MacKenzie disappeared into the girls' bathroom, she flashed me an evil grin over her shoulder and mouthed . . .

LOO-ZER!

And right now I'm feeling like one. Because thanks to MacKenzie, my life has been totally

TRASHED!

No pun intended ☹!!

WEDNESDAY, NOVEMBER 20

I've pretty much given up all hope of being in the talent show.

And I still don't have the slightest idea how I'm going to continue attending WCD.

When I saw Chloe and Zoey in gym today, I really wanted to apologize and try to explain everything before MacKenzie completely brainwashes them into believing all her lies.

But I didn't get a chance to talk to them because our gym teacher announced that we were going to be playing basketball.

Then she selected four captains to pick teams.

Unfortunately, I'm a very crummy basketball player and have NEVER made a basket in my entire life.

So I wasn't the least bit surprised when I was the

very last person to be picked out of the entire class.

OMG! Talk about HUMILIATING ☹!!

And as if being the last person wasn't BAD enough, the four team captains got into a heated argument over who was going to get "stuck" with me on their team.

It's no wonder I struggle with low self-esteem!

I was hoping that Chloe, Zoey and I would end up on the same team, but no such luck.

Anyway, the winning teams were going to earn an A while the losing teams had to take showers. This made me supernervous because I HATE showering at school.

I never knew that playing basketball could be so . . .

PAINFUL!

And when I asked my gym teacher if I could wear a helmet, shoulder pads and shin guards, she got an attitude about the whole thing and told me I just needed to hustle more and be a team player.

But what I really wanted to know was, HOW was I supposed to spend quality time writing in my diary when I was getting clobbered by that basketball every three seconds?!

By the end of the game I was sick of that ball. So when someone passed it to me, I just whipped it right over my shoulder without looking. I wanted to get rid of it so I could write in my diary.

But get this! I made the winning basket with only
two seconds left in the game.

Then everyone came running up to congratulate me!
And my teammates hoisted me up on their shoulders
like I was a hero and we had just won the state
championship or something.

WAY
TO GO!

?!

I had NEVER in my entire life seen people SO happy about NOT having to take a SHOWER!

While we were in the locker room, I was hoping to try to talk to Chloe and Zoey again.

But since their team had lost, they were stuck taking showers.

I quickly decided it would be more prudent to have a heart-to-heart with them at another time.

Besides, I just don't know what to say right now.

Other than the truth.

Which at this point is NOT an option.

OMG! I could NOT believe what happened in social studies today!!

The cruddy thing about being so depressed is that I hadn't really paid a lot of attention to my homework assignment.

I mean, HOW can you study when your entire world as you know it is crumbling around you?

To make matters worse, class participation is an entire third of our grade.

So you CAN'T just sit in the back of the room texting all your friends about how the class is SO boring you're sitting in the back of the room texting all your friends.

Since I wanted to improve my grade, whenever there was a question I knew the answer to, I tried FRANTICALLY to get the teacher's attention.

TEACHER: "Is it really warm and stuffy in the classroom today, or is it just me?!"

Hey! It was a QUESTION and I actually knew the ANSWER!

Of course, my teacher totally IGNORED me.

Like he always does when I know the answer.

Then we started discussing that social studies reading assignment that I'd ~~barely read~~ quickly skimmed.

TEACHER: "So, who can tell me how a democracy, a republic, a federal republic and a parliament are different from one another, AND name a specific country as an example of each. Okay! Let's see . . ."

I tried to avoid eye contact and hide behind my book while chanting over and over in my head . . .

But did it work?! NUH-UH!

TEACHER: "How about . . . Miss Maxwell?"

Of course I looked like a total IDIOT because I didn't know the answers to his seventeen-part question ☹!!

That's when I totally lost it and screamed,
"Um, excuuuuusse ME, Mr Teacher Guy! But can
I ask YOU a little question?! Why do you ONLY
call on me when I DON'T know the answer? It
seems a little DYSFUNCTIONAL or something,
if you ask me!"

But I just said that inside my head, so no one else
heard it but me.

When class was finally over, I was putting my
books in my backpack when the strangest thing
happened.

Violet came up and wanted to know if I was
still going to put together a band for the
talent show.

I just stared at her with my mouth wide open.

I could NOT believe she wanted to be in my band.

"Um, sure! I'd LOVE to have you on keyboard!" I
said happily.

Violet smiled and gushed, "Thanks, Nikki. This is a dream come true!"

That's when Theodore turned around and gave me this really weird look.

Although, to be honest, Theodore ALWAYS looks a little weird. By some fluke of nature, he could easily pass as SpongeBob's human twin brother.

"DUDE! You're putting together a band?!" he asked excitedly.

"Actually, YEAH! I am. But isn't your band already signed up for the talent show?" I asked.

Theodore's band, SuperFreaks, had totally ROCKED our Halloween dance. And according to the latest gossip, they were an inside favorite to win the talent show.

"Haven't you heard? MacKenzie convinced most of my bandmates to quit and join her stupid dance group. She told them the cheerleaders had crushes on them and were dying to be their dance partners. Now there are only two SuperFreaks left — me and Marcus," Theodore said sadly as his eyes filled with tears. "The rest of our guys have gone . . . to the, the . . . D-D-DARK SIDE!"

He was so upset, I actually felt sorry for him. I gave him a tissue and he blew his nose.

"I'm really sorry to hear that," I said, trying to look very sympathetic that he'd lost the majority of his bandmates to the Dark Side.

Boy, did THAT sound familiar!

"So . . . um, do you guys need a bass and lead guitar player?" Theodore asked hopefully.

"The jobs are YOURS!" I said happily.

I explained to them both that I'd already made arrangements to use the band room for practices and that maybe we could have our first practice tomorrow morning.

And since the deadline for entering the talent show was ALSO tomorrow, I'd sign us up first thing in the morning.

"Cool!" said Violet.

"Yes! VERY cool!" Theodore added.

That's when it finally occurred to me that we still had a major problem.

"Um . . . the only remaining issue, guys, is that we need a drummer. We can't do this unless we have a drummer." I felt like a balloon that had just had all the air let out of it.

Violet looked crushed. "You're right! We won't stand a chance! CRUD! My music career is over even before it got started!"

Theodore squinted his eyes and tapped his chin like he was doing a really hard geometry problem in his head or something. "Well, like I said earlier, the SuperFreaks' drummer has gone to the Dark Side.

But I know another guy I could ask. He said he was too busy to be in our band, but I'm thinking he might be willing to hang out with us just for a week or two for the talent show. He's really good, too."

"Really?!" I said, hopeful again. "Definitely ask him!"

I started thinking this crazy plan might actually work.

"Hey, we're IN IT to WIN IT!" I said, giving Violet and Theodore a high five.

Theodore

Violet

Me

"So, I'll see you both tomorrow morning, then!" I said as I grabbed my backpack and calmly walked out of the room.

But inside my head I was SO happy, I was doing my Snoopy "happy dance."

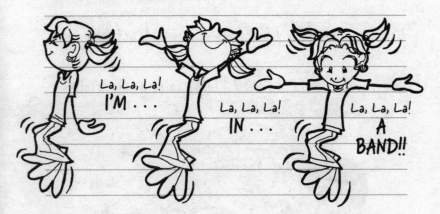

La, La, La!
I'M . . .

La, La, La!
IN . . .

La, La, La!
A BAND!!

OMG! I could have boogied all the way to my next class!

MacKenzie has convinced my best friends and Theodore's bandmates to join her dance group by cleverly brainwashing them.

And she has stolen my crush by flirting with him and pretending to be interested in photography.

But now I am about to make a comeback.

Starting today, I am going to put my time and energy into my new band.

And we are going to be FIERCE!

YEAH, BABY!!

I was so excited about my first band rehearsal, I barely slept last night. I got up extra early, grabbed a granola bar for breakfast and rushed right out the door.

Even though school didn't start for another hour and fifteen minutes, the halls were already noisy with ongoing practice sessions.

I was happy to see the main office was open, and I stopped in to fill out the paperwork to enter our band in the show.

Just as I was about to finish up, the LAST person I wanted to see walked in. Okay, make that the SECOND to LAST person.

With so much other stuff going on, I just didn't have the energy to deal with him right then. I tried my best to hide behind my backpack so he wouldn't see me.

ME, TRYING TO HIDE
BEHIND MY BACKPACK

BRANDON

But it didn't work.

"Hey, you!" Brandon said with a big smile. He seemed pleasantly surprised to see me.

"What's up?" I answered, coolly nonchalant. Like I HADN'T just been trying to figure out how to crawl into my backpack and zip myself up.

"Nothing much. I just stopped in to say hi to a friend," he answered.

I quickly glanced around the office. No students were in there except us.

"Well, no one has come in since I've been here. . ." I said, trying to sound like I didn't care.

"Hey! Aren't YOU my friend?!" Brandon teased.

"Oh! You meant ME?! Sorry! I just thought. . ."

I bit my lip and blushed profusely as he stared at me with that look on his face. The one that can send me into a severe and debilitating case of RCS (Roller-Coaster Syndrome) in mere seconds.

I was like, "WHEEEEEEEEE!!" But I just said that inside my head, so no one else heard it but me.

I tried to regain my composure. "So, what are YOU doing here so early? Other than saying hi to a friend."

"Actually, I'm here for a talent show practice. I kind of got talked into it at the last minute."

I felt like someone had just dumped a gallon of ice water down my back.

Brandon?! In the talent show. . . ?!

Suddenly it occurred to me that if MacKenzie needed a dance partner, HE'D definitely be her FIRST choice. I mean, why NOT?!

But HOW could Brandon just let MacKenzie wrap him around her little finger like that?!

"Oh, reeeally? How . . . quaint!" I said through my clenched teeth. "Sooo, I take it you're dancing with your little . . . Picture Pal."

Brandon blinked and looked slightly confused. "Picture Pal? I don't have a . . . Oh! You mean MacKenzie?"

DUH!!

I gave my best fake smile. "Yeah, I just hope you survive your BIG MAC attack!"

Then I very obviously rolled my eyes at the ceiling.

Brandon laughed, leaned over and playfully nudged me with his elbow. "Nikki, you KILL me! Big Mac attack?!"

Personally, I didn't see what was SO dang funny. "Yeah, you two have been inseparable lately. All that . . . PHOTO BONDING."

Brandon laughed even harder. WHY?! I was NOT trying to be funny!

Finally he glanced at his watch. "Well, I better get going. See you . . . later."

I couldn't control myself. It was like I had diarrhea of the mouth or something. "Good luck with your Camera Cutie. I hope you both . . . um . . . break a leg!"

Brandon shook his head and gave me a weak smile. "Uh, thanks. I guess."

Then he turned and walked out of the office. I stared at him until he disappeared down the hall.

I replayed our conversation in my head.

Picture Pal? Big Mac attack? Photo bonding? Camera Cutie?

I cringed at my words. WHY did I always act so CRAZY and IRRATIONAL around that guy?!

No wonder he preferred hanging out with MacKenzie. He probably thought I was a NUT CASE!

I tried to put the two of them out of my mind. I had more important things to worry about, like band practice. Which, BTW, was supposed to officially start in two minutes.

I needed to finish the entry form and hand it in or we wouldn't be able to perform.

I had completed all the questions but one: NAME OF ACT?

Hmmm. We still needed to come up with a slightly edgy, cool-sounding name.

Something like . . . Purple . . . Poison . . . Fuzzballs . . . of . . . Doom? NOT!!

Or maybe Hungry . . . Plastic . . . Screaming . . . Toenails? NOT!!

So for the name of my band, I wrote in "Actually, I'm not really sure yet."

I handed the form to the secretary, grabbed my backpack and rushed down the hall towards the band room.

I had no idea what to expect.

We barely had eight days to select a song and learn it well enough NOT to make complete FOOLS of ourselves.

Otherwise known as

MISSION: IMPOSSIBLE.

Theodore plays cello in the school orchestra, and his best friend, Marcus, plays violin. They are both "first chair" which means they are the best at their instruments.

I was really impressed how they had gone from playing classical music to Top 40 tunes. Although it probably wasn't that hard, considering the fact that the two of them have a combined IQ higher than the rest of the entire school.

These guys make ME (a self-proclaimed dork) seem like a social butterfly.

Their idea of a stimulating conversation is debating whether the *Star Wars* lightsaber or the *Star Trek* phaser is the more technologically advanced weapon.

Violet is pretty much a loner who spends hours

and hours practising classical piano pieces. I've heard she has played in competitions all over the nation and won.

But playing pop music on the keyboard is a whole different thing, and I was a little worried she'd make Bieber sound like Bach and Miley sound like Mozart.

Our biggest problem, however, was that we didn't have a drummer, and that really worried me. How could we have a good chance at winning without one?!

By the time I got to the band room, everyone was already there and warming up.

I was totally surprised to see the back of a guy stooped over, adjusting a drum set. Did we actually have a drummer??!!

Then he turned around and smiled and waved at me, and I practically FREAKED!

Theodore had recruited **BRANDON?!**

I didn't even know Brandon played the drums!

I just stood there like an idiot staring at him and then the other band members, and then at him and then the other band members, and then at him and then the other band members, and then at him again.

This went on for what seemed like FOREVER!

And then Brandon kind of shrugged and said, "Um, Nikki, are you okay?! You kinda look like you're having a seizure or something."

I was like, "Who, ME? Nothing's wrong! I mean, why would you think something's WRONG? I'm totally fine!"

But mostly I was in SHOCK because I could NOT believe that I FINALLY had my very own band and my CRUSH, Brandon, was actually there playing drums.

I was like, "SQUEEEEE!!" ☺!!

Then we started talking about music, and I learned a lot of new stuff.

Like, musicians can play "by ear" or from sheet music.

The really supertalented ones can just listen to

a song and figure out how to play it in a few minutes.

Otherwise, you can use sheet music and read the notes for the songs, which is a lot easier to do.

Well, guess what? My band is SO talented, they didn't even need sheet music!

I suggested the old-school song "Don't Stop Believin'" because it's one of my dad's favorites. I thought it was funny how everyone was into it again because it was on a TV show.

Each of them quickly figured out their own part, and within ten minutes they were playing it together.

It was absolutely AMAZING to see and hear!!

Then Theodore told me they were finally ready for me to sing along and handed me a microphone.

I was shaking so badly, I thought I was going to drop it.

Of course I muttered, "Testing, one, two, testing, one, two! Um, is this thing on?" like a total idiot.

It was on, and my voice was really loud and clear.

Just like the butterflies in my stomach.

After they played the intro to the song, I closed my eyes, took a deep breath and started singing along.

We actually sounded really, really good. Well, really good for a band that had only been together for, like, thirty minutes.

When we finally finished the song, Theodore, Marcus, Brandon and Violet raved about how well I sang, especially without having practised or anything.

However, my little secret is that I've sung and danced to that song a million times.

In front of my mirror, using my hairbrush as a microphone.

The most surprising thing to me was that Brandon is SUCH an awesome drummer!

But he made me supernervous because he was, like, STARING at me the entire time.

I blushed and smiled at him. And then he blushed and smiled at me.

And when he thought I wasn't looking, he stared at me AGAIN!

So I blushed and smiled AGAIN! And he blushed and smiled too!

All of this staring, blushing and smiling went on, like, FOREVER!!

Now I'm starting to wonder if Brandon actually likes me as MORE than just a friend!!

And if he DOES, I'll seriously just DROP DEAD from severe shock and extreme happiness!

I even wrote a poem about him.

DEATH BY DRUMMER
By Nikki Maxwell

Thump—thump!
Goes your bass drum.
Like the relentless
Pounding of my lovesick heart.

Rat—tat—tat!
Goes your snare drum.
Like fragile bullets of hope
Piercing the cloud of pure nothingness that is me.

Crash! Bang! Crash!
Goes your cymbal.
Like me very clumsily
Knocking over that row of folding chairs
Because you make me SO insanely nervous.

Does your skin sparkle in the sunlight?
Probably not!
But your intense eyes smother me
And your gentle smile fatally wounds
my jaded soul.

My heart skips a BEAT
and suddenly . . . STOPS!
Overwhelmed by the awesomeness that is YOU!
Give me liberty!
Or give me . . . DEATH by drummer!

Before I knew it, the hour had passed and it was
time to leave for our first class.

Since the talent show is next Saturday, we decided to practise one hour before school and one hour after school every day for the entire week.

Which means I'll be spending a lot of time with Brandon ☺!! SQUEEEEEE!!

Being in this talent show is one of the most exciting things I've ever done in my entire life.

I was really happy and in a supergood mood the rest of the day.

Even when I saw MacKenzie and Jessica whispering and giving me the evil eye during lunch.

I was like, WHATEVER!

My new band is beyond FABULOUS!!

And now I have a really good shot at winning that scholarship.

☺!!

SATURDAY, NOVEMBER 23

I planned to spend the entire evening brainstorming ideas for my band.

The show is less than one week away, and we still need to come up with a name, select a song and figure out what we're going to wear.

Unfortunately, my parents announced that it was Family Movie Night and insisted that I come down and watch a rented movie with them.

My inner child screamed, "NOOOOOOOOO!!"

OMG! Talk about pure TORTURE!!

It's ALWAYS a SUPERold movie that's already been rerun a million times on TV like *Raiders of the Lost Ark, Star Wars,* or *The Lord of the Rings.*

My dad says he loves renting them to see all the scenes that were cut out of the original movie release.

What he FAILS to realize is that the directors cut those scenes for one of two reasons.

Reason number one: They were BAD. And reason number two: They were BORING.

I was like, "Dad, are you kidding? Making us watch these movies for the seventh time is AWFUL enough. But we also have to see two additional hours of really BAD and BORING scenes. Personally, I'd rather get a big bowl of popcorn and watch the kitchen tap drip."

But I just said that inside my head, so no one else heard it but me.

And my mom's favourites are oldies like *Honey, I Shrunk the Kids*; *Freaky Friday*; *Legally Blonde* and *13 Going on 30*.

Which I HATE slightly less than Brianna's favorites: *Princess Sugar Plum Saves Baby Unicorn Island!* parts 1, 2, 3, 4, and 5. Princess Sugar Plum's voice sounds like a chipmunk on helium. . .

"Please don't worry, all you cute, liddle, adorable baby unicorns. I, Princess Sugar Plum, am here to save you all! AGAIN! For the fifth time! All because I'm CUTE, LIDDLE and ADORABLE, just like all of YOOOU!!"

Family Movie Night movies are SO LAME, I'd love to

borrow Princess Sugar Plum's pink candy-cane magic
wand and transport myself to the moon.

WHY?

SO IT WILL BE
PHYSICALLY IMPOSSIBLE
FOR MY PARENTS TO
FORCE ME TO WATCH
THIS RUBBISH!!

That's why!!

I'm just saying. . . !!

☹!!

SUNDAY, NOVEMBER 24

Tonight my parents went out to dinner and asked me to babysit Brianna.

At first I was like, NO WAY ☹! But I finally agreed to do it after they offered to pay me.

I need the money to make some supercool T-shirts for all my bandmates.

We're going to look AWESOME wearing matching T-shirts with jeans when we perform in the talent show.

Am I NOT brilliant ☺?!

Anyway, the worst thing about babysitting Brianna is that she always takes TOTAL advantage of the situation.

And, since I'm getting paid, she acts like I'm her little PLAYMATE-FOR-HIRE or something.

Which means for the past two hours I've valiantly suffered through a very off-key live performance of Brianna and Miss Penelope singing the hit "Single Ladies"!

GAH!

"Nikki, I'm gonna be Miss Penelope's backup singer when she goes on her world tour!"

AND I've attended a Princess Sugar Plum tea party dressed like someone's great-grandmother, with a doll and a motley crew of stuffed animals. . .

You would think that after I suffered through these playtime indignities, Brianna would have appreciated it and NOT given me such a hard time at dinner.

But NOOOO!!

Mom left me specific instructions that Brianna could NOT leave the dinner table until she'd eaten ALL her broccoli.

So Brianna just sat there pouting and slapping her broccoli around on her plate with her fork like she was playing miniature golf or something.

I told Brianna she was going to have to either eat that stuff or sit there another forty-five minutes until her bedtime. Of course she got an attitude about the whole thing.

I left the table to put my dishes in the dishwasher.

And when I got back, I was shocked to see that Brianna's plate was completely clean and she had this angelic smile on her face that went from ear to ear.

You could practically see her halo.

I was more than a little suspicious.

"Brianna, are you SURE you ate all your broccoli?!"

She nodded and just kept smiling like an insane clown. But I was NOT about to be outsmarted by a six-year-old.

That's when I demanded that she open her mouth. Well, not HER mouth, exactly . . . Miss Penelope's mouth.

But surprisingly, Brianna had not stashed her broccoli in there.

So I gave her a big hug and told her how proud Mom was going to be of her.

She didn't say a word and just continued to smile like she was in a Miss America contest.

Unfortunately, NOW I know why!

I had tucked Brianna into bed for the night and was feeding the fish in Dad's aquarium when I spotted these strange chunks of green gunk floating around in the water.

At first I thought it was some kind of deadly, flesh-eating algae or something.

But upon closer examination it looked exactly like . . . Wait for it . . . Wait for it . . .

CHEWED-UP BROCCOLI!! UGGGHHHH!! OMG!

I almost lost my meat loaf right there on the living room carpet.

I screamed at the top of my lungs:

"BRIANNA! You SPAT broccoli in the fish tank?!! Get down here and clean up this mess! RIGHT THIS MINUTE!!"

I was so MAD, I could have STRANGLED her!

I knew she was just pretending to be asleep.

Which meant I was the one STUCK cleaning HER slimy broccoli gunk out of the aquarium.

It was the GROSSEST thing EVER!

227

Babysitting that evil little munchkin is such a humongous PAIN!

As a matter of fact, the next time my parents ask me to watch her so they can go out to dinner, I'll pay *THEM* $30 to STAY HOME and ORDER a &!@#$% PIZZA!!

I'm just sayin'!

At least I have the money for our T-shirts.

All we need to do now is come up with a really cool name for the band and select our song.

☺!!

Today my
WORST
NIGHTMARE came true ☹!

After an insanely boring morning at school, it was finally time for lunch.

I grabbed my lunch tray and was making my way over to table nine when I noticed the strangest thing.

The ENTIRE cafeteria seemed to be staring at me and whispering and snickering.

At first I thought maybe toilet paper got stuck to my shoe from my trip to the bathroom.

Or maybe a humongous booger was dangling from my nose.

But then I spotted MacKenzie across the room, glaring at me all evil-like with this huge smirk on her face.

And right next to her were a bunch of CCPs crowded around her superexpensive hot pink designer notebook computer laughing their . . . um . . . behinds off.

That's when I got this really, really BAD feeling.

My thoughts were racing as I collapsed in my seat at the lunch table.

Could she have. . . ?!

Would she have. . . ?!

Did she DARE. . . ?!

Well, I finally got the answers to my burning questions when Matt looked at me and yelled . . .

Of course the whole cafeteria cracked up laughing.

My stomach was churning, and I had totally lost my appetite.

I kept thinking, OH. NO. SHE. DIDN'T!!

But MacKenzie HAD!!

I was SO humiliated! I blinked back my tears and tried to swallow the huge lump in my throat.

I wanted to run away, but at that moment I was too upset to move.

So I just stared at my tuna noodle casserole.

I was about to dump my tray and leave when MacKenzie sashayed over to my table.

"I heard you and some other DORKS from SuperFreaks started a new band. What are you calling yourselves, DORKALICIOUS?!"

"MacKenzie, why did you tell everyone about the Queasy Cheesy video?! I kept my part of the deal," I said, still fighting back tears.

"So what if you did! Now that Chloe and Zoey are on my team, I just have to make sure I don't have any major competition. And since I heard your little band was half decent, I figured now was the perfect time to let the world know what a talentless loser you are. SORRY about that!"

WHY in the world had I EVER trusted that girl?!

"Hey, Maxwell, I wanna see you do your Queasy Cheesy dance!" Matt continued to taunt me from the jock table.

"Matt, I wanna see *YOU* do some personal hygiene," someone retorted. I whipped my head around and was stunned to see Chloe and Zoey standing on the other side of the table. When had they got there?

Chloe slammed Matt with yet another insult as she slid into the seat to my left. "Dude, even your flies are starting to drop dead from the odour!"

"Yeah! You're SO nasty I wouldn't slap your face with somebody else's hand," Zoey huffed as she took the seat to my right.

I almost fell over from shock. It seemed like we hadn't sat together at lunch for ages.

"Are you okay?" Chloe asked, and gave my shoulder a squeeze. "We heard about that YouTube thing."

"We actually thought you and your sister were adorable!" Zoey said, smiling.

I didn't believe that "adorable" part for one minute.

I looked like a total idiot in that video. And it was VERY obvious that Chloe and Zoey were just lying through their teeth to try to make me feel better.

Which was one of the NICEST things they have ever done for me!

They are the sweetest BFFs EVER! I don't deserve friends like them.

I was just about to apologize to Chloe and Zoey and try to explain everything when MacKenzie started shrieking like a lunatic.

"Chloe! Zoey! WHAT are you two doing? I specifically instructed ALL my dancers to sit together at table four!!"

"Um, you guys don't have to sit with me. We can talk later, okay?" I muttered.

MacKenzie rolled her eyes at me. "Besides, Nikki is about as talented as a toilet plunger! OMG! That video was painful to watch."

"Well, at least I'm not a shallow, fashion-obsessed diva like you. If your brains were dynamite, you wouldn't have enough to blow your nose!" I shot back.

"OH, PUH-LEEZE! You're just jealous because you're not in MY dance group. Everyone knows we're going to win!" MacKenzie spat. "Chloe! Zoey! It's either Nikki or ME! You better decide right now."

Slowly they both stood up. I felt HORRIBLE that they were choosing MacKenzie. But I really didn't blame them.

I was the biggest DORK in the school, and she was the biggest DIVA.

"Well, I'm glad to see you girls have finally come to your senses. At least you know a phony friend when you see one," MacKenzie said smugly.

"It wasn't a hard choice at all," Chloe said.

"I agree. There's so much phony baloney that if I had bread and mustard, I could make a sandwich!" Zoey exclaimed.

I just stared at my two friends. I felt like I had been kicked in the stomach.

Then Zoey placed her hands on her hips and took a step toward MacKenzie.

"We heard every word you said to Nikki. And you know what? You REALLY need to get over yourself! It's hard to breathe up in here with your stank attitude!"

I could NOT believe Zoey had just said that!

Chloe folded her arms and nodded.

"Yeah, I've had quite enough, *chica*. You can't treat our friend like that and get away with it. Oh, and one other thing . . . I QUIT!!"

"ME TOO!" Zoey said.

"What?! You CAN'T quit!" MacKenzie screeched.

"WE JUST DID!" Zoey said.

"Yeah, what part of 'I quit' do you NOT understand?!" Choe asked.

MacKenzie trembled with rage, and the water from the bottle in her clenched fist sprayed everywhere!

"FINE! I don't need you, anyway! Just stay out of my way, or you'll be sorry!" MacKenzie snarled. Then she stomped back to the CCP table.

I was SO happy my BFFs had chosen me over MacKenzie. And they had stood up for me too!

We did a group hug right there at table nine.

"Oh, well. I guess we won't be in the talent show after all," Zoey said.

"Yep! That's showbiz!" Chloe quipped, and gave us jazz hands.

"Hey, I have an idea!" I said. "Why don't you guys join our band? We're practising after school today. We could use two more singers!"

"I don't know. . ." Chloe said.

"Yeah," Zoey agreed, "I'm kind of sick of all the drama."

"Please!" I begged. "It would be just like our Ballet of the Zombies days! How FUN was that?!"

"Yeah! That WAS pretty awesome!" Chloe conceded.

"Even though we got a D," Zoey added wistfully.

"Well, before you say NO, at least come to our practice after school today," I pleaded.

"I guess that sounds fair," Chloe said.

"I can't wait to hear you guys!" Zoey gushed.

I could see MacKenzie staring at us from across the cafeteria and whispering to Jessica.

But none of that mattered.

I finally had my BFFs back!

☺!!

We had a BLAST at band practice yesterday!

Chloe and Zoey were superimpressed. And since they already knew everyone, they fitted right in.

So now they're official members and will be dancing and singing backup ☺!

I can hardly believe my BFFs and I are actually going to perform onstage together.

SQUEEEEEEEEEEEEEEEEE ☺!!

MacKenzie's master plan to keep me out of the talent show had failed miserably. And now I was about to become her worst nightmare: stiff competition!

So it was poetic justice when we agreed to call our band

DORKALICIOUS

(courtesy of MacKenzie!).

We even wrote an original song that was inspired by MacKenzie's little insult.

It all started when Violet crossed her arms and smugly announced, "Hey! I'm a dork and PROUD of it!"

Then we started joking about which of us was the BIGGEST dork. The guys were like, "Can you please stop goofing around?"

Then Zoey said, "Actually, we're not goofing around. We're doing . . . um . . . vocal warm-ups."

"Yeah, and vocal warm-ups are VERY important!" Chloe added as she playfully gave the guys the stink eye.

That's when Zoey started singing, "Tryin' to fit in at my school, but kids keep telling me a dork ain't cool."

And Chloe sang, "Whenever the teasing gets vicious. . ."

"I remind myself I'm super DORKALICIOUS!" I chimed in.

We burst into giggles and gave each other high fives!

The guys just smirked and rolled their eyes at us. Then the three of them started whispering to one another.

I knew they were up to something, and I figured they were going to try to outdo us.

And I was right!

244

THEY started clowning around TOO!

The next thing we knew, they were dancing, singing and frontin' like hard-core rappers:

> "Dork, nerd, geek, freak
> Is all you see
> But just back off
> And let me be ME!"

We all laughed so hard, our sides hurt.

The WEIRD thing was that their song had a catchy melody and a really great beat. It was the kind of song that gets stuck in your head for the entire day.

Even though it was supposed to be a joke, us girls actually LIKED it. Of course, the guys thought we were NUTZ!!!

But they finally agreed to let us try to turn it into a real song. While Violet, Theodore, Brandon and Marcus worked on the music, Chloe, Zoey and I quickly grabbed a piece of paper and finished writing the words.

By the end of our practice session, we had a very cool, original song about not fitting in at school and being who you really are.

I have to admit, it isn't about superserious stuff like lost love or saving the world.

But it's OUR song, and it expresses how we feel. That's the most important thing.

Now that we finally have a name for our band, I was able to get started on our T-shirts.

Blasting my fave tunes, I threw a one-person paint-'n'-glitter party that lasted until midnight.

There is only one word to describe my designer creation: "DORKALICIOUS" ☺!

With everything that's been going on lately, I've been SO distracted. I'd probably forget my head if it wasn't attached to my shoulders.

Everyone in the entire school seems to know about DORKALICIOUS!

Students have even started congregating outside the band room door to listen to us practise.

It's almost like we're a real band with real fans.

And NOT just a group of dorky friends who love music and have only been playing together for less than a week.

The latest gossip is that MacKenzie's dance group is no longer a slam dunk to win the talent show.

Which I guess is good news for us.

Especially for me, since winning the talent show scholarship is the ONLY way I can stay at this school.

I thought about telling Chloe and Zoey about my dad and everything else, but I think it'll just complicate matters.

The last thing I need is them questioning my true
motives AND our friendship AGAIN.

But at the same time, keeping all these secrets feels
really wrong.

ARRGGH ☹!! I have to ask myself:

WHAT WOULD SCOOBY DO?!!

Anyway, today is our last day of school before the
Thanksgiving break.

The dress rehearsal for the talent show is on
Friday, and then Saturday is the big day.

PLEASE, PLEASE, PLEASE let me
win so I can get that scholarship!!

The good news is, even if I DON'T win, I probably
WON'T have to worry about transferring to a new
school.

WHY?

Because when my parents find out everything, they're going to KILL ME!

And it's probably ILLEGAL to transfer a DEAD BODY to a new school. . .

Is this 911? We have an emergency! Some parents just dropped off a new transfer from Westchester Country Day. Only, I don't think she's breathing . . .!!

THURSDAY, NOVEMBER 28

Today is THANKSGIVING DAY ☺!

I LOVE, LOVE, LOVE this holiday.

Mainly because I get to eat enough food to feed the entire cast of *Big Time Rush*.

Brianna and I helped Mom finish up the cooking while my dad drove to the airport to pick up my grandma.

Having Grandma over for the weekend is a real treat because we haven't seen her since we moved here last summer.

She said there was NO WAY she was going to miss seeing me sing in the talent show, and she was coming even if she had to ride her Segway the entire three hundred miles.

And she's CRAZY enough to do it!

GRANDMA

Grandma says all her friends have Segways too. And for fun, they get together and ride around town like an elderly motorcycle gang swigging bottles of Pepto-Bismol and squirting denture cream on the door handles of parked cars.

Grandma's a little wacky! Actually . . . A LOT wacky!

But Mom says that's because she has an eccentric personality and a zest for life. Personally, I think all that's just a polite way of saying she's SENILE.

But you GOTTA LOVE HER ☺!!

Here she is with her three adorable poodles named Larry, Moe and Curly.

GRANDMA →

Anyway, our Thanksgiving dinner was WONDERFUL!

GRANDMA

After everyone had stuffed themselves, Dad lit the fireplace in our living room and we all sat around and played a game of charades.

It was my brilliant idea to do famous singers, and we took turns drawing names out of a hat.

When it was Grandma's turn, we almost DIED laughing.

OMG! She did a KILLER impression of Lady Gaga!

After our game was over, Grandma gathered us around and hugged each one of us. Her eyes started to water as she announced that she had something really important to say.

"I guess I should tell you the real reason I wanted to spend Thanksgiving here. I'm getting on in age, and one day soon I'm going to be leaving here and going on a VERY long trip. I know we're going to miss each other, but I want everyone to know how much I love you all. So I'm giving you your Christmas present today. Mainly because I'm NOT going to be here with you physically for the upcoming holidays. But I WILL be here in spirit!"

That's when Dad got really emotional, and tears started streaming down his face. "Mom, we love you too. But please don't talk about dying and leaving us!"

OMG! It was SO sad, even I sniffed a couple of times.

That's when Grandma turned around in her chair and rolled her eyes at my dad like he was a COMPLETE IDIOT.

"For Pete's sake! When you were a baby, your dad must have dropped you on your head a few times too many. Who's talking about DYING?! Gladys, Beatrice and I are flying out to Las Vegas for two weeks, and we're leaving next Wednesday. From there we're doing a road trip to Hollywood to see a taping of Betty White's show and _The Price Is Right!_ We won't be back until AFTER Christmas."

We all breathed a HUGE sigh of relief.

Grandma continued, "Anyway, before I leave, I want to give you all an early Christmas present! It's a priceless family heirloom that has been passed down through generations of Maxwells since 1894. Or was it 1984? One of those years. I forget which. Anyway, it's my most prized possession."

She went to the closet and pulled out a large Christmas present topped with a shiny red bow.

That's when it occurred to me that if her heirloom

was a superexpensive antique, maybe my parents could sell it on eBay, use MY portion to pay off my tuition, and STILL have thousands of dollars left over.

Maybe Grandma coming to visit and giving us our present a month early was the answer to my prayer.

NOT!

When we opened the box, inside was a SUPERold iron bucket with a large handle on the side.

My dad's eyes lit up and then quickly filled with tears again.

"MOM, you shouldn't have!!" he gasped. "It's Grandma Gertrude's ice-cream maker. She used to make me ice cream with it when I was a little boy!"

I was like, JUST GREAT! So much for my idea of selling it to pay my tuition bill ☹!

Our so-called priceless heirloom was basically a piece of JUNK!

By next month we'd probably be using it as a makeshift recycling bin. Then during our annual spring cleaning Mom would pay the junk hauler to take it and a few other of Dad's garage sale treasures (like his paddle-less canoe) to the city dump.

Grandma handed my mom a piece of paper that had the Maxwells' secret ice-cream recipe written on it.

"I'd LOVE some creamy, delicious, Maxwell family ice cream for dessert. Anyone else?" Grandma beamed proudly.

Brianna got so excited, she started dancing around. "Yaaay! I scream! You scream! We all scream for ICE CREAM!"

"What a great idea!!" Mom said as she herded us all into the kitchen. "I think making ice cream together would be a wonderful Family Sharing Time! Come on, everyone. FUN, FUN, FUN!"

I was like, oh crud! "Family Sharing Time"? Again? Noooooo! ☹!

Making homemade ice cream sounds like a harmless, family-friendly activity. Right?

But NOT with an antique, cast-iron, hand-cranked ice-cream maker.

Things got REALLY complicated when Dad showed Brianna what he used to do for fun when he was her age.

When Mom wasn't looking, he and Brianna tried to SNEAK a few licks of ice cream that had spilled over the sides.

Who'd have thunk such an old-fashioned gadget like that could reach FUTURISTIC SUBZERO TEMPERATURES?!

THE MAXWELL FAMILY
MAKING HOMEMADE ICE CREAM

AAAAHHH!

HALP! I think my thung iz thuck on da thide of thiz iceth keam thingy!!

Can you find the TWO things very WRONG with this picture?! I'm just sayin'. . . !!

After this little fiasco, I now know for certain who Brianna inherited her LACK of intelligence from!

I thought for sure their tongues were going to freeze solid, snap off, fall on the floor and shatter into a million little pieces.

Luckily, Dad and Brianna only ended up with a mild case of frostbite. And a severe, but temporary, lisp.

I was surprised Mom's ice cream was so DELISH!

But every time that image of Dad and Brianna popped into my head, I'd start laughing so hard that ice cream would shoot right out of my nose and give me a really painful BRAIN FREEZE.

Hey, I wonder if it's true that if you take a hot shower right after a brain freeze, your brain will melt and you'll turn into a CCP. Hmmmm . . .

Anyway, we had a very HAPPY THANKSGIVING!

☺!!

FRIDAY, NOVEMBER 29

Today was the talent show rehearsal at the WCD High School auditorium.

It's a fairly new facility that seats two thousand people. Just the thought of performing in front of such a large crowd gave me butterflies.

The guys set up all our equipment while Chloe, Zoey and I did vocal warm-ups.

Violet hung out with us too and kept telling us how great we sounded.

The high school student producer of the talent show was Sasha Ambrose, a supertalented senior who won the competition two years in a row when she was in middle school.

The butterflies in my stomach were quickly replaced by a cold, heavy lump of dread when I saw MacKenzie backstage, whispering to Sasha and pointing at ME ☹!

All the talent gathered in the auditorium and waited excitedly for Sasha to assign dressing rooms and give us our order of performance.

There was a total of eighteen acts, and she called them up one by one, EXCEPT Dorkalicious.

After all the others were dismissed to go backstage, she finally motioned for us to have a seat in the front row.

Of course we were all concerned about why we hadn't been called up along with the others.

Sasha pulled out our entry form, read it over, and slowly shook her head. "So, what's the name of your group?"

"Dorkalicious!" we all answered at once.

"Well, unfortunately, I have some bad news. It's been brought to my attention that the deadline for all entry forms was Friday, November twenty-second. And it specifically states here in writing that failure to submit a completed form will result in disqualification from the show."

I didn't have the slightest idea why she was telling us all of this.

I had *personally* completed our entry form right

there in the school office and handed it in BEFORE the deadline.

We all started to panic and talk at once.

Sasha raised her hand, signaling us to quiet down. "Listen, people, I'm sorry, but the rules are the rules!"

"I don't understand," I said. "I filled out the form and turned it in myself. How can we be disqualified?!" I was on the verge of tears.

"Yeah, it WAS turned in on time," she answered. "The problem is that it's INCOMPLETE! It doesn't say on here that the name of your group is Dorkalicious."

She handed the entry form to me, and everyone crowded around to read it for themselves.

In the blank where it said "Name of act" I had scrawled, "Actually, I'm not really sure yet".

My heart sank! Everyone shook their heads in shock and disbelief.

I crumpled the entry form and jammed it into my pocket as tears flooded my eyes. "I am SO sorry, guys!" I muttered. "I guess she's right. It's all my fault. I don't know what to say. . ."

"I CAN'T believe it!" Violet exclaimed. "Nikki, how could you forget to do something so important?"

I just shrugged my shoulders and stared at the floor.

That's when Brandon came to my defence.

"Well, we have to remember that this whole band thing was kind of thrown together at the last minute. We hadn't even picked a name yet."

Sasha started talking into a headset, and suddenly the house lights dimmed.

The curtains opened to reveal the first act, which was a seventh-grade rap group dressed in fuzzy dog costumes. They were performing the song "Who Let the Dogs Out?"

I hoped it was supposed to be a comedy act.

"This is SO unfair!" Chloe groaned.

"There has to be something we can do!" Zoey moaned.

"That's showbiz!" Violet said sarcastically.

Sasha shot us a dirty look and covered the mic on her headset. "In case you haven't noticed, I'm trying to put on a show here. Take it out in the hall. Please!"

We sighed and slowly shuffled out of the dark auditorium. Then the five of us threw a private pity party for Dorkalicious.

Everyone looked SO disappointed. It was heartbreaking.

I could NOT believe I had let them all down like that.

I was the most horrible friend EVER!

I didn't know what to say, so I just apologized again.

"Guys, I'm REALLY, REALLY sorry. I can't believe we won't be performing after all those long hours of practise. I wish there was a way to make this up to you. . ."

Everyone gave me a small smile and shrugged it off.

"Hey, so what! They only kicked us out of the talent show! It's NOT the end of the world," Chloe said, smiling goofily and doing her jazz hands.

"And with the Dragon Lady running things, there's no way we're getting backstage to take down our equipment," Theodore said. "I'm outta here! Pizza, anyone?"

"Yeah, we can always get our stuff after the show

tomorrow," Marcus added. "Pizza sounds GREAT to me!"

Everyone started to cheer up a bit and agreed to hang out at the pizza place across the street. Which was a good idea since our parents weren't scheduled to pick us up from practice for another two hours.

But I still felt horrible and my stomach was churning. Just the thought of pizza made me feel ill.

"Sorry, guys, but I'm exhausted. I think I'm gonna head home."

"Come on, Nikki, don't beat yourself up!" Brandon pleaded.

"Yeah, we gave it our best shot!" Violet added.

"But more than anything, we had fun hanging out and practising together, right?!" Chloe said, giving me a hug.

"I guess so. Listen, you guys go ahead. I'm gonna call

it a night, 'kay? Eat a piece of pizza for me," I said, smiling weakly.

Finally they gave up trying to talk me into going with them.

Even though everyone was disappointed by our disqualification, they were trying to be good sports about it.

I do NOT deserve friends like these!

I could hear them laughing and joking as they headed out the front door.

I found a pay phone and called home for a ride. As I sat at the front door waiting for my mom to arrive, I started to feel even worse.

Winning a talent show scholarship was my only hope for staying at WCD.

And now even that is gone.

I buried my face in my knees and cried.

Suddenly I heard footsteps approaching.

I quickly brushed away my tears and wiped my runny nose on my sleeve.

"Nikki, you look horrible!" MacKenzie said, sneering. "OMG! What kind of lip gloss are you wearing? Oh, that's not lip gloss . . . it's SNOT!"

I was like, JUST GREAT! I rolled my eyes at her.

"I heard Dorkalicious got disqualified. Too bad!
Thank goodness Jessica had office duty and was
able to check your entry form to make sure you
weren't cheating."

"MacKenzie, I wasn't trying to cheat. We just
hadn't selected a name yet. . ."

"Well, look at the good side! At least now you
won't have to get up onstage and publicly humiliate
yourself. AGAIN! And with both Dorkalicious AND
SuperFreaks out of the way, it will be an easy win
for me and my dancers!"

"MacKenzie, you are a dismally vain, self-absorbed
blonde abyss of seething wretchedness!" I blurted out.

She smiled at me wickedly. "You say that like it's a
BAD thing!"

Then she took out her lip gloss and slathered on a
fresh layer.

"Anyway, I didn't come out here to talk to YOU. Now that Brandon is no longer in the talent show, Sasha needs him to handle the photography."

"Unfortunately, he left a few minutes ago."

MacKenzie eyed me carefully, trying to figure out if I was lying or not.

"Well, if you see him, please give him the message that Sasha and I need to talk to him."

"Since when am I your personal secretary? If you have a message for Brandon, you can tell him yourself."

MacKenzie placed her hands on her hips and flashed another evil smile. "Crush much? Get a clue, hon. You want Brandon? Dial 1-800-YOU-WISH!!" Then she spun around and sashayed down the hall.

I just HATE it when MacKenzie sashays.

Just then my mom pulled up, and I dragged myself out to the car.

"So, practice got out early?" she asked.

"Yeah, something like that," I mumbled.

As soon as I got home, I rushed up to my room and collapsed on my bed.

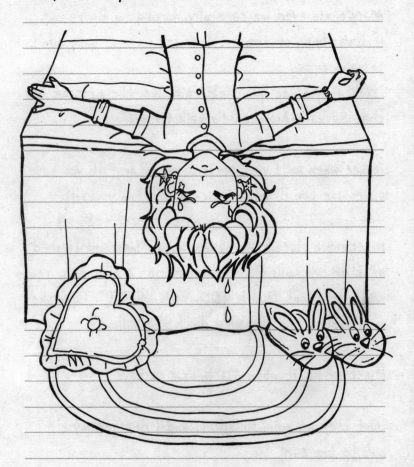

I just lay there in the darkness, pondering my massively cruddy situation.

I am SUCH a LOSER!

And a PATHETIC friend!

I want to believe that things are so bad, they can't get any worse.

But I already know it's going to get worse.

A LOT worse!

Tomorrow morning I am going to have to tell my parents the truth about EVERYTHING! ☹!!

SATURDAY, NOVEMBER 30

When I finally woke up, it was almost noon.

Knowing that I was going to have to face my parents made me feel a little nauseated.

On top of that, the sun was shining in my eyes and I had a splitting headache.

I was surprised to see that I still had on my clothes from last night. I grabbed my pillow, groaned and buried my head under it.

Suddenly there was a knock on my door. But I ignored it.

Most Saturday mornings, Brianna and Miss Penelope wake me up. But today was my lucky day.

Before I could yell "GO AWAY!" Brianna, Miss Penelope AND my grandma all barged in.

A TRIPLE dose of INSANITY could easily destroy the very weak grip I held on my pathetic reality.

It was enough to make me want to jump out of my bedroom window screaming.

"Wake up! Wake up!" Brianna screamed. "Me, Grandma and Miss Penelope need you to help us make some homemade ice cream!"

My grandma sat next to me on the bed and tickled me. "Time to get up, Miss Lazy Bones!"

"Please, Grandma. Stop! I don't feel so good! And I'm exhausted!"

"Well, no wonder. How can you get a good night's sleep with all this junk on your bed? Backpack, book, sneakers and. . . ?"

She picked up a crumpled piece of paper that had fallen out of my pocket.

". . . assorted litter. Is this any good, or can I throw it away?" she said, opening it up and reading it. She slid her glasses down her nose a bit and squinted.

"Oh, THAT thing. It's nothing. Just toss it!" I muttered.

I shoved my head back under the pillow, hoping Grandma and Brianna would take the hint and get lost.

"Are you sure, honey? This looks like it might be important. Hmmm? WCD Talent Showcase Entry Form. So, the name of your band is Actually, I'm Not Really Sure Yet. Now, that's a bit odd, don't cha think?"

"Miss Penelope says she's looking for chocolate cupcakes. Any cupcakes in here, Nikki?!" Brianna said as she rummaged through my sock drawer.

That's when I peeked out from under my pillow.

"NO, Brianna! There are no cupcakes inside my sock drawer. And Grandma, NO! That's NOT the name of my band! Like, how totally STUPID would that—"

I stopped midsentence.

Inside my head, my brain was screaming, "OMG! OMG! THAT'S IT!!"

I'd just had the most FANTASTIC idea!

Maybe there was still hope for our band after all.

I was so happy, I hugged Grandma.

"I LOVE YOU, GRANDMA!" I giggled as I jumped up and down on my bed.

She climbed up and joined me. "I love you too, sweetheart! I'm glad you're feeling better."

"Hey! What about MEEEEEE?!" Brianna screeched. "And Miss Penelope. We wanna jump too!"

All four of us held hands and jumped on my bed like it was a trampoline or something.

I promised to help make the ice cream as soon as I'd made a few phone calls.

So Grandma and Brianna rushed downstairs singing "Girls Just Want to Have Fun" at the top of their lungs and really off-key.

I could hardly wait to call Chloe and Zoey.

When I told them my idea for getting us back into the talent show, they thought it was brilliant.

Next we called Violet, Brandon, Theodore and Marcus and made plans to meet with Sasha to update her about our new status.

My final task was to make some major design adjustments to our band T-shirts.

Later that evening everything went as planned and we cornered Sasha backstage.

I smoothed out our crumpled entry form as best I could and handed it back to her.

However, before Sasha could read it, MacKenzie came rushing over. "Nikki Maxwell, WHAT are you doing here? Sasha has already told you Dorkalicious is disqualified!"

"MacKenzie, we're not entering the talent show as Dorkalicious," I said happily. "Our entry form is correct."

MacKenzie looked totally confused. "WHAT?! If you're not Dorkalicious, then who are you?!"

She obviously didn't have a clue.

Sasha read over our entry form and slowly nodded. "Yeah, it makes sense. If that's the name of your band, I guess you guys are back in the show. . ."

"WHAT! How can they be back in the show? Nikki, you can't get away with this!" MacKenzie screamed, stomping her foot like a toddler having a temper tantrum or something. "It's not FAIR!!"

"Later, MacKenzie!" I said. "Break a leg!"

Only I REALLY meant it.

Well, okay. I meant it just a little.

The word got around quickly that we were back in and that the competition was going to be brutal.

After the show started, we sat in a dressing room watching all the other acts on a television monitor.

There were magic acts, dance groups, bands, singers and musicians, and most of them were really good.

Winning the talent show was NOT going to be easy.

After about an hour and a half the assistant stage manager finally took us backstage and told us to wait in the wings since we were going on next.

MacKenzie's dance group was performing, and I had to admit they were awesome.

They wore sequined jumpsuits and pretty much danced their butts off to a medley of the latest pop tunes.

The crowd went wild.

Since our band was added to the lineup at the last minute, we were the last act to perform.

Violet and the guys were entering from stage left, and Chloe, Zoey and I were entering from stage right.

While we were waiting to go on, suddenly my stomach started doing double somersaults.

I must have been having a panic attack or something because my brain was screaming stuff like, "WHAT are YOU doing?! You CAN'T go out there and sing in front of all those people! What if you MESS UP?! Your life will be RUINED!!"

But I wanted that scholarship so badly that I didn't have a choice.

Chloe and Zoey must have sensed my fear because they each took my hand and squeezed it and told me I was going to do fine.

My knees still felt really wobbly. But it was great to know that if they actually gave out and I fell over, Chloe and Zoey would be there to drag me across the stage and stick the microphone in my hand.

They are, like, the BEST friends EVER!

I cannot begin to explain what it felt like to hear the crowd when the announcer introduced us. . .

"And our next act is a band made up of Nikki, Chloe,

Zoey, Brandon, Violet, Theodore and Marcus. Please welcome to the stage . . .

ACTUALLY, I'M NOT REALLY SURE YET!!"

I really LOVED our new name! It sounded edgy and professional, just like those real bands on MTV!

We quickly walked onstage and took our places.

I nervously glanced out at the audience and squinted, trying to spot faces I knew. But because of the glare of the bright stage lights, the crowd was just a big massive blur of darkness, noise and excitement.

Which actually was a good thing, because not seeing a million people staring back at me made me feel less nervous.

I looked over my shoulder and Brandon gave me a huge smile and a thumbs—up.

He then did four taps with his drumsticks, launching Violet, Theodore and Marcus into the intro of the song.

OMG! They sounded SO good! I had to remind myself it was my four friends playing that music live, and NOT a song blasting on my iPod.

Chloe, Zoey and I started our dance routine just the way we had practised it.

Then I smiled at my BFFs, took a deep breath, and sang the first note.

At first it felt a little shocking to hear my own voice so loud and clear. But I just tried to relax and enjoy our performance.

By the time we got to the chorus . . .

"Dork, nerd, geek, freak
Is all you see
But just back off
And let me be ME!"

293

. . . I could see the first two rows had got up on their feet and were dancing along.

When we finally finished our song, the crowd cheered like crazy and we got a standing ovation.

They actually loved us!

Chloe, Zoey and I hugged one another as our musicians exchanged fist bumps and high fives.

I was SO hoping we were going to win. We HAD to win!!

All the acts quickly filed back onstage and lined up around us.

As MacKenzie and her dance group crowded in right next to us, she smiled sweetly at Brandon. "You guys were awesome! Good luck!"

"Thanks! Good luck to you too!" he said politely.

Then MacKenzie turned and looked at me like I

was something she had scraped off the bottom of her shoe.

Which didn't surprise me one bit.

As the judge, Mr Trevor Chase, took the stage, the tension was so thick you could cut it with a knife.

"As you are aware, ALL the talent here was very, very good. I encourage each of you to continue to hone your craft. But tonight there can only be one winner. And the winner . . ."

I held my breath and chanted inside my head, Please let it be us. Please let it be us. Please let it be us!

". . . of the tenth annual WCD Talent Showcase is . . . **Mac's Maniacs!**"

MacKenzie shrieked! Then she hugged Jessica as all her dancers crowded around hugging one another.

I was SO disappointed, I felt like crying.

It wasn't the losing part that made me feel so bad, but the fact that I was going to have to leave WCD and my friends.

I think the rest of my band was a bit surprised we lost, but they were being really good sports about it.

After we left the stage, we all hugged one another too. And everyone told me I sang really well.

"Nikki, this was SO fun!" Violet gushed. "We didn't win. But, hey, that's . . ."

"SHOWBIZ!" all seven of us shouted, and then erupted into peals of laughter at our little joke.

But deep down inside, I felt really horrible knowing I was going to have to say goodbye to everyone in a few days.

My eyes started to tear up, but I didn't want my friends to see me crying.

"Um, my throat is a little dry. I'm gonna run out to the hall to get a drink. I'll be right back, 'kay?" I announced, and took off before anyone had a chance to join me.

I went straight to the girls' bathroom and splashed water on my face. I cringed at the thought of having to tell my parents all the crazy stuff I'd done.

Suddenly the bathroom door opened and MacKenzie rudely brushed past me in a hurry.

"Excuse you!" she hissed as she whipped out her makeup. "I have a photo shoot to do."

I just rolled my eyes at her.

"Too bad you lost! I tried to warn you not to waste your time. At least Jessica and I will FINALLY get to have lockers next to each other when YOU transfer to a public school! Ever since your dad got hired as the exterminator, our school has been overrun with bugs.

"Besides, you're way too poor to pay that tuition bill that you got in the mail last week, so you—" MacKenzie got this really funny look on her face and bit her lip. Then she took out her lip gloss and nervously slathered on a thick layer.

I wanted to tell her to keep her nose out of my business and that she had no idea what she was talking about. Although, to be honest, she knew EXACTLY what she was talking about because there was no WAY we could pay that tuition bill and—

Suddenly it hit me. MacKenzie did know EXACTLY what she was talking about, but HOW was that possible? How did she know about my bill, and why was she now squirming and avoiding eye contact?

I put my hands on my hips and stared right into her beady little eyes. "So, MacKenzie . . . HOW did you know I got a tuition bill? Or did your BFF Jessica also send YOU a copy of the PHONY BILL that she sent ME?!"

"Well, she's just the office assistant in her free periods. She would NEVER, like, mail out stuff to people, actually. . ." MacKenzie stumbled as her cheeks flushed.

I could not believe my ears. For the past two weeks my life had pretty much been one gigantic, continuous nightmare as I desperately tried to figure out how to pay that tuition bill.

Then I'd practically had a meltdown dealing with the mental anguish of a possible transfer to a new school.

ONLY to FINALLY find out it was just another of MacKenzie's cruel pranks??!!

Right then I was SO angry I wanted to grab one of MacKenzie's $495 suede Prada ballet flats and shove it right down her throat. I took a step towards her.

"YOU and Jessica sent me a phony tuition bill?! I've been worried sick about how my parents were going to pay it. How could you do that?!"

MacKenzie nervously batted her eyes at her perfect reflection in the mirror and then snapped the cap back on her lip gloss.

"I don't have the slightest idea what you're talking about."

"MacKenzie, you are such a liar!"

"And besides, even if we DID send you a phony tuition bill, you don't have any proof! Do you? . . . LOSER!!"

With that, she turned and sashayed out of the bathroom.

I just HATE it when MacKenzie shashays!

Although, to be honest, I was SUPERrelieved to find out that bill was from HER and NOT the school.

I felt like I was finally waking up from a two-week-long nightmare.

Well, I learned my lesson, that's for sure!

No more secrets! I was going to tell Chloe and Zoey about my dad and my scholarship the first chance I got.

And once the entire school knew about it, I would no longer have to lie awake nights wondering if and when MacKenzie was going to drop the bomb.

It was like a heavy weight was lifting off my shoulders even as I thought about it.

Just then Chloe and Zoey rushed into the bathroom out of breath.

"Oh, there you are! We've been looking everywhere for you!" Zoey panted. "MacKenzie told us you were in here."

"OMG! You are NOT going to believe what just happened!" Chloe's eyes were huge!

"After you left," Zoey continued, "Trevor Chase came over and congratulated us. He said he wanted to let us know that *15 Minutes of Fame* features unpolished amateurs going through boot camp to get better. He said we sounded really professional and were actually too good to be on his show. Can you believe THAT?! He said he won't start filming the new season until next fall, and that's when MacKenzie's group will get to audition. But he wants to work with us RIGHT NOW! Nikki, he LOVED our song and wants us to release it ASAP!"

"WHAT! Are you kidding?! NO WAY!" I sputtered.

"Yep! He says he wants to meet with all of us and our parents after the holidays and that he'll be in touch!" Chloe continued.

The three of us started screaming and did a group hug!

I could NOT believe that people all over the world might actually be able to hear OUR song!

And if we made any money, I could use MY portion to FINALLY buy myself a NEW PHONE ☺!!

Back in the auditorium, I was talking to my parents when Principal Winston came up and congratulated me.

I was praying that he wouldn't mention that bug extermination fiasco.

But he did!

Apparently, my parents had run into Principal Winston and his wife at that restaurant last Sunday. He and Dad had chatted and then arranged a meeting for next Saturday to evaluate the WCD bug problem.

Thank goodness my dad had NOT been fired after all. I was SO relieved!

I never thought in a million years I'd actually be happy he was the WCD exterminator.

But more than anything, I'm SUPERgrateful that Dad arranged my scholarship. I guess I didn't really appreciate it until I thought I had lost it.

Anyway, I already know the ONLY bugs Dad and Principal Winston are going to find at WCD are in a jar in MacKenzie's locker.

But I've learned my lesson the hard way, courtesy of MacKenzie.

I will NEVER, EVER stick my nose in my dad's business again! And that's a PROMISE!

So I just kept my big mouth shut about the WCD bugs.

After we'd changed out of our band T-shirts, Chloe, Zoey and Violet went back to the dressing rooms to pack up the rest of our stuff.

Brandon and I sat in the second row of the auditorium, which was now pretty much empty.

He told me that renaming our band Actually, I'm Not Really Sure Yet at the last moment was pure genius.

But I admitted that it was my grandma who had given me the idea.

He also said he was really proud of me and that I was such a good singer, I could be a star.

I was like, yeah right, a not-so-talented pop star!

So, we were just sitting there facing each other, and he kind of stared at me for what seemed like FOREVER.

I blushed and my stomach got all fluttery inside.

OMG! I just HATE it when he does that to me.

Then I smiled. And he smiled back at me with this sort of shy look on his face.

I almost FREAKED when Brandon kind of leaned forward a little until we were, like, ten centimetres apart.

My heart was pounding so hard I could hear it in my ears.

Because for a second I thought that maybe he was going to . . . you know . . . !!!

SQUEEEEEEEEEEE ☺!!!

But that's when Brianna suddenly popped up from the row right behind us and leaned over our seats and shoved her fist right in Brandon's face and shouted:

"WHAT'S UP, DUDE? MEET MISS
PENELOPE! SHE WAS BORNED
FROM A PEN! AND SHE SAYS
YOU HAVE COOTIES!!"

I could NOT believe Brianna actually did that.

OMG! I was SO embarrassed.

But mostly I felt SUPERGIGGLY and INSANELY HAPPY because everything had worked out.

So I grabbed Miss Penelope and gave her a big, fat, sloppy kiss.

Which totally grossed her out.

"Her" being Brianna, not Miss Penelope.

And of course Brandon and I both cracked up.

I guess he knows by now that I'm just weird like that.

OMG!

I am SUCH a DORK!!

☺!!

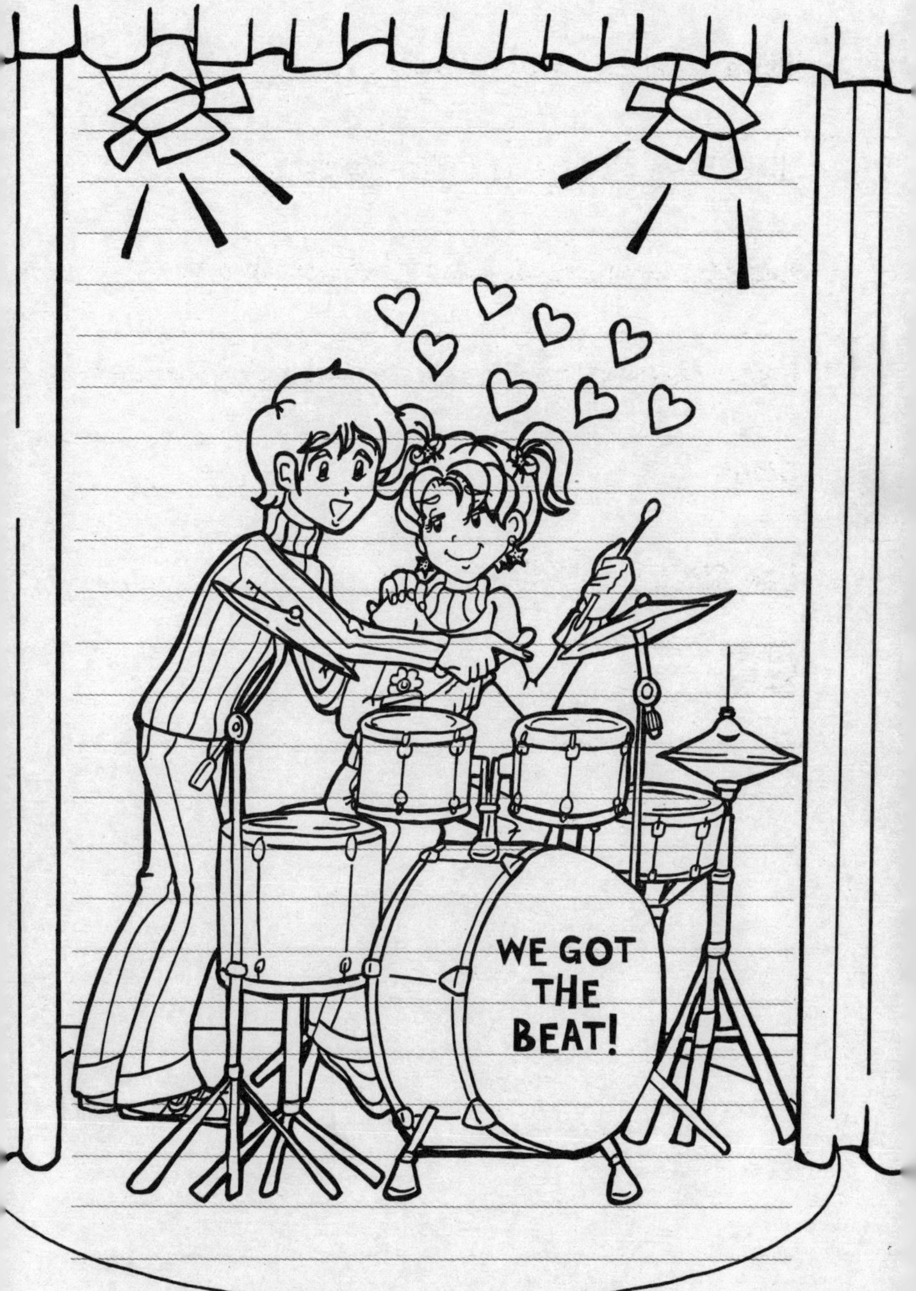
WE GOT
THE
BEAT!

Nikki's Tips for a perfect Skate-a-thon
#1 Find a worthy cause to skate for
#2 Have lots of fun by teaming (major points
up with BFFs Chloe and Zoey if Brandon
loves it too!)
#3 Make sure you can actually skate...

Can Nikki transform from a

dork-on-ice to an ice-princess?

Turn the page to find out in

Dork Diaries: Skating Sensation...

OMG!

I have never been so EMBARRASSED in my entire life!!

And this time, it WASN'T at the hands of my snobby, lip-gloss-addicted enemy, MacKenzie Hollister.

I still can't figure out why my very own sister, Brianna, would humiliate me like this.

It all started earlier this afternoon, when I noticed my hair was greasier than a supersized order of fries. I needed either a shower or an emergency oil change. I'm so NOT lying.

I hadn't been in the shower more than a minute when SOMEONE started pounding on the bathroom door like a maniac. I nervously peeked out of the shower and was like, "What the. . . ??!!"

"How much longer are you going to HOG the bathroom?" Brianna yelled. "NIKKI. . . ?!"

BAM!! BAM!! BAM!!

"Brianna, stop banging on the door! I'm in the shower!"

"But I think I left my doll in there. She and Miss Penelope were having a pool party and—"

"WHAT?! Sorry, Brianna! I do NOT want to hear about your poo in the potty."

"NO! I said 'POOL PARTY'! I need to come in and get my doll so I—"

"I CAN'T open the door right now. GO AWAY!!"

"But, Nikki, I gotta use the toilet! Really BAD!"

"Just use the one downstairs!"

"But my doll isn't in the bathroom downstairs!"

"Sorry, but you can't get your doll right now! Wait until I'm done with my shower!"

Unfortunately, one minute later. . .

317

NIKKI, OPEN THE DOOR! YOU HAVE A
PHONE CALL! NIKKI?!

"You need to open the door so you can talk on the phone!"

BAM!! BAM!! BAM!!

Did Brianna think I was stupid or something? I was NOT about to fall for the old open-the-bathroom-door-because-you-have-a-very-important-telephone-call trick.

"Sure, Brianna! Just tell 'em I don't feel like talking right now."

"Um, hello. Nikki says she doesn't want to talk right now . . . I don't know? Hold on. . . ! Nikki, the person wants to know when to call back."

BAM!! BAM!! BAM!!

"NIKKI?! The person wants to know when—"

"NEVER! Tell them to call back NEVER! And they can DROP DEAD for all I care. All I want to do

319

right now is TAKE A SHOWER!! So, please, Brianna!
Just LEAVE ME ALONE!!"

"Um, hello. Nikki said to call her back never! And
drop dead too! Uh-huh. And guess why. . . ?!"

That's when it occurred to me that just maybe
someone WAS actually on the telephone. But WHO?
I hardly ever get any telephone calls.

"Because YOU'VE got COOTIES! That's why!"

Brianna laughed like a criminally insane clown.

I was a little worried because that insult sounded
really . . . familiar. She'd said the exact same thing
to someone just yesterday. But there was no way
that person would EVER call ME!

Suddenly I got this really sick, panicky feeling
deep inside, and my mouth started screaming,
"NOOOOOOOO!"

I grabbed a towel and scrambled out of the

shower, soaking wet and completely covered in soap suds.

"Okay, Brianna!!" I whisper-shouted. "GIVE. ME. THAT. PHONE. NOW!"

But she just stuck her tongue out at me and continued blabbing on the phone like she was talking to a long-lost friend from school.

Nikki ALWAYS hogs the bathroom! My mom yells at her because she's so messy. And when she wakes up in the morning, she looks superscary. But that's because she has hairy legs and crusty eye-boogers!

I could NOT believe Brianna was telling all of MY personal business like that. How DARE she?! "Brianna! Hand over that phone or else. . . !"

"Say 'pretty please with sugar on top'!"

"Okay! Give me the phone, pretty please with sugar on top!"

"NO! Too bad, so sad!" Then that evil little munchkin stuck her tongue out at me (AGAIN!) and continued blabbing on the phone.

"Anyway, my friend Miss Penelope sneaked some of Nikki's new perfume. She loved how it smelled even though she doesn't have a nose. We sprayed it on stuff to make it smell pretty. Like my feet, the rubbish bin in the garage and that dead squirrel in Mrs Wallabanger's backyard!"

Hijacking my phone calls was bad enough. But she's been fumigating things with my Sassy Sasha perfume as well?! I wanted to STRANGLE her!

"Give me that PHONE, you little BRAT!" I hissed.

But she just said, "Toodles!" and took off running.

Chasing Brianna was VERY dangerous!

OMG! At one point I slipped and almost slid right down the stairs and into the kitchen. That would have been a first-degree rug burn for sure! OUCH! It made me cringe just thinking about it!

I finally cornered Brianna and was just about to tackle her, when she dropped the phone and ran screaming down the hall. "Help! Help! The slime mould in the shower grew arms and legs and is trying to SLIME me! Somebody call 911!"

I picked up the phone and tried to act coolly nonchalant, and not like I was standing there . . .

1. In a bath towel

2. Dripping wet AND

3. Covered with enough soap suds to wash a small herd of very dirty llamas.

I cleared my throat and answered in my cutest, most perky-sounding voice . . .

"UM . . . HELLO-OO!!"

324

"Nikki? What's up! It's me, Brandon!"

I could NOT believe what my ears were actually hearing. This was the very FIRST time my crush had ever called me! I thought I was going to have a heart attack right there on the spot.

"Hi, Brandon! I'm really sorry. That was my little sister. She makes up the craziest stuff. Actually."

"No problem! So . . . I'm just calling to let you know I'm inviting a few friends over for my birthday in January. I was hoping you, Chloe and Zoey would come."

That's when I fainted. Okay, ALMOST fainted.

"Wow! Um, well! I, er . . . Can you hold on for a minute? There's something I need to do."

"Sure. Do you want me to call you back?"

"Nope. It'll only take a minute."

I carefully covered the phone with my hand and then

proceeded to have a massively severe attack of RCS, also known as . . .

ROLLER COASTER SYNDROME!!

WHEEEE!

Okay. So maybe I overreacted just a little bit.

It wasn't like Brandon was asking me out on a date or something. I wish!

Anyway, after we finished our telephone conversation, I pinched myself really hard just to make sure I wasn't dreaming. OUCH!! Yep, I was awake! Which means CHLOE, ZOEY AND I ARE INVITED TO BRANDON'S PARTY ☺!!!

It's gonna be a blast! I can hardly wait!

Especially considering the fact that I'm the biggest dork at my school and pretty much NEVER get invited to parties.

OMG! I JUST HAD THE MOST HORRIBLE THOUGHT ☹!!! . . .

After his conversation with Brianna, Brandon probably thinks I'm some kind of, um . . .

HAIRY-LEGGED . . .

CRUSTY-EYED . . .

FREAK!!!...

Why would he want to hang out with ME?!!

There is NO WAY I can go to Brandon's party!

I'm going to call him back right now and tell him I can't come.

DUH!! I completely forgot! I STILL need to finish my SHOWER! So I'll call him afterwards.

And then I'm going to crawl into a very deep hole and . . . DIE of EMBARRASSMENT!

☹!

MONDAY, DECEMBER 2

I'm totally dreading seeing Brandon in school today.

It's hard to believe that just a couple days ago we were rocking our school's talent show together in our band, Dorkalicious (also known as Actually, I'm Not Really Sure Yet). Yes, it's a crazy name and a long story.

He even gave me lessons on his drum set. It seemed like we were FINALLY becoming good friends.

But then Brianna the Brat RUINED everything!

I'm surprised Brandon even bothered to invite me to his party. I bet he only did it because he feels sorry for me or something.

I wanted to talk to Chloe and Zoey about all of this during gym, but I didn't get a chance to. Mainly because the entire class was buzzing about nabbing a really cool, FREE T-shirt for this show called *Holiday on Ice*.

But after our gym teacher practically shattered my eardrums, all I really wanted was for her to accidentally SWALLOW that stupid whistle!

ME →

Then she made a big announcement. . .

"Okay. Listen up, people! We'll be starting our ice-skating section next week. Grades will be based on the skill level each student successfully masters. However, as part of our Westchester Country Day holiday tradition, and to encourage community service, all eighth-grade students participating in the Westchester *Holiday on Ice* charity show on December thirty-first will get to practise their routines during class and receive an automatic A. Yes, folks! You heard that right! I'll be giving out As like sweets to support this great cause. Just let me know whether you'll be doing the skills testing or the ice show. Now hustle up to the table and grab a free *Holiday on Ice* T-shirt. Then get started on your warm-up exercises."

That T-shirt thing did *NOT* go so well for me.

By the time I got to the table, all that was left was size XXXXXL. MacKenzie, of course, looked like she was ready for the summer cover of a teen magazine.

MACKENZIE, LOOKING CUTE AND
TRENDY IN HER NEW T-SHIRT

ME, LOOKING LIKE AN UGLY, SHAPELESS BLOB

I was so . . . DISGUSTED ☹!

Of course MacKenzie took one look at my T-shirt and started giving me unwanted fashion advice. "Nikki, do you want to hear my idea for how to make your T-shirt stylishly elegant, yet practical?"

"No, MacKenzie. Actually, I don't."

"Just add three inches of white lace around the hem, a veil and a bouquet of flowers, and you can use it as a WEDDING dress! Then all you have to do is PAY some FREAKISHLY ugly guy to marry you!"

I could NOT believe she actually said that right to my face like that.

"Thanks, MacKenzie!" I said, smiling sweetly. "But where will I find a freakishly ugly guy? Oh, I know! Do YOU have a twin BROTHER?!"

Only MacKenzie would be STUPID enough to make a wedding dress out of a five-sizes-too-big T-shirt. But that's because her IQ is LOWER than an empty bottle of nail polish!

MACKENZIE'S VERY STUPID IDEA FOR A DESIGNER T-SHIRT WEDDING DRESS

ME → ← VEIL

BRIDAL BOUQUET

XXXXXL T-SHIRT

LACE AT HEM

SUPERCUTE SHOES →

Calling MacKenzie a "mean girl" is an understatement. She's a GRIZZLY BEAR with a French manicure and blonde hair extensions.

But I'm not jealous of her or anything. Like, how juvenile would THAT be?

Anyway, I was excited about skating in class. The last time I did it was back in, like, third grade, and it was a lot of fun.

Chloe said we'd be skating at the ice hockey arena at WCD High School.

Apparently, the *Holiday on Ice* show is a big deal, and only students in grades eight to twelve can participate to raise money for their favourite charity. The show donates $3,000 to every charity that a skater, skating pair, or group sponsors.

We were about to start our exercises when suddenly Chloe got this crazy look in her eyes and started doing jazz hands.

"Hey, you guys! Guess what I'm thinking!"

But I already knew. Lately, she's been obsessed with this new book called *The Ice Princess*.

It's about a girl and a guy who have been best friends forever.

She's training to be a world-class figure skater

while he's working towards a spot on the Olympic hockey team.

Just as they're about to fall in love, they discover that their ice arena is the secret hideout of the Deadly Ice Vambies, half-vampire and half-zombie beings whose supernatural ice-skating abilities grow more and more powerful every time they eat a double bacon cheeseburger.

"There is no reason why WE can't be Ice Princesses too! Just like Crystal Coldstone!" Chloe sighed dreamily.

Personally, I could think of TWO very good reasons why we COULDN'T be like Crystal.

First, we haven't been training with a skating coach for the past twelve years. Second, it was going to be really difficult to slay Deadly Ice Vambies on school nights and still get our homework done on time.

Zoey got this wistful, faraway look in her eyes.

"How ROMANTIC! And hockey players ARE kind of cute! Besides, I'd much rather make up a really cool skating routine and get an A than do boring skills testing. We'll have a blast! How about it, Nikki?"

"I don't know, guys. Skating for a charity is a really big responsibility. They're going to be depending on us for money to help keep their doors open. And what if something goes wrong?"

"Come on, Nikki!" Chloe whined. "We're not good enough to skate individually, and skating pairs require a girl and a guy. But the three of us can skate as a group. We can't do this without you!"

"Sorry, but you're going to have to find someone else!" I said, shaking my head.

"But we want YOU!" Zoey pleaded.

"Yeah, and don't forget! We were there for you when you needed us for the talent show," Chloe argued. "BFFs help each other!"

Okay, I have to admit Chloe had a good point about the talent show. But it wasn't like I'd promised them my firstborn child in exchange for them singing backup.

Then Chloe and Zoey shrewdly resorted to a sophisticated tactic that effectively rendered me helpless. . .

PLEASE, PLEASE, PLEASE, PLEASE
PLEASE, PLEASE, PLEASE, PLEASE!!

BEGGING!!!

"Okay, guys! I'm IN! But you can't say I didn't warn you!" I sighed.

We sealed the deal with a group hug.

"Great! Now all we have to do is find a local charity to skate for," Zoey said.

"Unfortunately, that's going to be the hardest part," Chloe said. "All of the high school kids have been signing up charities for a few weeks now. So we're getting a really late start. But I'm pretty sure we'll find one," she added cheerfully.

"OMG!" Zoey squealed. "This will be just like our old _Ballet of the Zombies_ days! Only we'll be getting an A instead of a D."

Actually, I kind of like that part too. It is going to be great to finally get an A in gym ☺!

Fortunately, ice skating DOESN'T involve embarrassing armpit stains, painful stomach cramps, or getting whacked in the head by a ball, like most of the stuff we are forced to do in gym.

And all of our work is going to be for a really great cause that will help the community.

But most importantly, I'll be making Chloe and Zoey superhappy by allowing them to live out their dreams.

We decided to skate to "Dance of the Sugar Plum Fairy" since it has a holiday theme. And we figured being fairy princesses would be superexciting and glamorous.

So I'm not going to stress out about this whole *Holiday on Ice* thing.

As long as I have my two BFFs by my side, everything is going to work out just fine.

I mean, how HARD can figure skating be?!

☺!!

TUESDAY, DECEMBER 3

Today in social studies we discussed career goals.

But since I plan to attend a major university to become a professional illustrator, I decided to spend the hour writing in my diary instead.

I felt it was the right thing to do since teachers always nag us students to use our class time wisely.

Most of the kids had not given much thought to their futures.

But my friend Theodore Swagmire III was totally obsessing over it.

And it didn't help that the class snickered when he shared his plans for the future. I felt a little sorry for him. He's one of the dorkiest guys in the school.

So, being the very kind and supportive friend that I am, I decided to encourage Theo to pursue his goals in life:

The GOOD news is that our little chat made Theo feel a lot better ☺!!

The BAD news is that he decided to start saving his allowance to buy a magic wand ☹!

Anyway, after class was over, Theo asked me if I was planning to come to Brandon's party in January. I wanted to tell the truth and just say no.

But instead, I made up an excuse. And not just a run-of-the-mill flimsy excuse. It was a totally unbelievable, embarrassingly STUPID one.

"I was planning to come. But I found out I had, um . . . an appointment to . . . take my sick . . . um, unicorn . . . to the . . . vet, actually."

Theo looked superconfused and scratched his head. "You have a unicorn?"

I wanted to say, "Hey, Wizard Boy! I probably got MY unicorn from the same place you're getting YOUR magic wand!" But I didn't.

Then in biology class, my very cruddy day turned into a complete DISASTER!

Brandon and I said hi to each other, but that was about it. The entire hour he just kind of stared at me with this perplexed look on his face.

He was probably imagining me as some kind of CRUSTY-EYED, HAIRY-LEGGED BEAST!

← ME

MacKenzie took full advantage of the situation and would NOT shut up!

I almost PUKED on my lab report when I heard her ask Brandon if he thought her Berry-Sweet-'n'-Flirty lip gloss colour matched her flawless complexion.

I could not believe she actually had the nerve to ask him something so ridiculously VAIN.

Especially when EVERYONE knows MacKenzie's so-called flawless complexion is from U-PAY-WE-SPRAY Tanning Salon at the mall.

That pukey-orange tan they sprayed on her is so tacky. Personally, I think she looks like a sunburned Malibu Barbie.

Then MacKenzie got all giggly and said, "Oh, by the way, Brandon, I heard you're having a party."

I was like, "Yeah, MacKenzie! And you'll ONLY be HEARING about it, because you're NOT invited!"

But I just said that inside my head, so no one else heard it but me.

I was shocked by what that girl did next!

She tried to HYPNOTIZE Brandon into inviting her to his party by flirting with him and twirling her hair AROUND and AROUND and AROUND her finger.

Just watching her made ME dizzy.

Thank goodness our teacher interrupted her. "MacKenzie, if you have time to chitchat in class, please go to the back of the room and clean out all of the rat cages. Otherwise, PLEASE. SIT. DOWN!"

MacKenzie practically RAN back to her seat.

OMG! It was SO funny! She totally deserved it.

But now she's giving ME the EVIL EYE from across the room like it was MY fault she almost got stuck doing rat-poop duty.

Anyway, I'm still convinced Brandon gave me a pity invitation. He probably didn't want to hurt my feelings.

I plan to tell him tomorrow that I can't make it to his party because I have another activity planned for that exact same time.

WHAT will I be doing?

Sitting on my bed in my pyjamas, STARING at the wall and SULKING!!!!!!! ☹!!

WEDNESDAY, DECEMBER 4

This morning I was feeling kind of down.

Even Chloe and Zoey noticed and asked me if I was okay. But I decided NOT to tell them about my mega-embarrassing phone conversation with Brandon. Especially after they went on and on about how EXCITED they were about his party.

On my way to lunch I decided to stop by my locker and drop off my backpack.

I was beyond surprised when I opened my locker door and a NOTE fell out!

At first I thought it was from Chloe and Zoey and they were trying to cheer me up or something.

But then I read it. Like, THREE TIMES!

OMG! I thought I was going to have a meltdown right there in front of my locker. . .

HI NIKKI,

CAN YOU MEET ME
IN THE NEWSPAPER
ROOM DURING LUNCH
TO TALK?

— BRANDON

I had no idea what Brandon wanted to talk to me
about.

My heart was pounding as I peeked inside the
newspaper room. I immediately recognsed his shaggy
hair behind a computer monitor.

"Nikki!" Brandon smiled, waved, and gestured for me
to come over.

Like an idiot, I looked behind me to make sure he wasn't talking to some other, um . . . Nikki.

HI, BRANDON. DID YOU WANT TO TALK TO ME ABOUT SOMETHING?

"Yeah. Actually, I do." That's when I noticed Brandon looked a little nervous too.

"Well! HERE I AM!" I blurted out all cheerful-like and louder than I meant to.

"Okay, um, I talked to Theo yesterday, and he said you can't come to my party."

GULP!

Brandon talked to . . . THEO?!

OH! CRUD!

I just kept smiling stupidly as Brandon continued. "He said something about you having to take care of a, um, sick unicorn?"

Just great! NOW Brandon was going to think I am a crusty-eyed, hairy-legged, SCHIZOPHRENIC HYPOCHONDRIAC!

"Really? Theo told you that?" I blinked my eyes all

innocentlike and laughed nervously. "That's . . . quite hilarious, actually. Theo's got a big imagination. Just like my little sister. She's as cute a button, but you can't believe a word she says. Especially if it's about . . . ME!"

"Yeah, tell me about it." Brandon laughed. "I wish I had a dollar for every time Brianna told me I have cooties." Suddenly he stared at me so intensely it made me squirm. "Nikki, you didn't seriously think I actually believed any of that stuff Brianna said about you, did you?"

"OMG! Of course not! Like, how immature would THAT be?" I giggled nervously. "Actually, Chloe, Zoey and I can't WAIT to come to your party."

Brandon broke into a big grin. "Cool! You had me worried there for a minute."

"So, what are you working on right now?" I asked, trying to change the topic.

I leaned over and peeked at his computer screen.

I saw snapshots of the cutest puppy and kitten.

"AWWW!" I gushed. "They're ADORABLE!"

"Those two are from the Fuzzy Friends Animal Rescue Centre. These pictures are going to run in the *Westchester Herald* next week."

"Wow! Impressive. Does the animal centre pay you to do that?"

"Nope. I guess you could say I volunteer my time. I want to be a veterinarian one day, so I really enjoy working with animals. Even though photographing them can be pretty challenging."

"Well, I think it's great that you take the time to help out. Sounds like fun!"

"It is. Hey! Why don't you come volunteer with me on Friday? I could use your help."

"Okay! That would be VERY cool!"

Brandon brushed his bangs out of his eyes and gave me a crooked smile.

I suddenly felt very nervous, giddy, and . . . nauseous.

That's when he kind of stared at me and I stared back at him.

Then we both smiled and blushed.

All of this staring, smiling and blushing seemed to go on, like, FOREVER!

Brandon and I spent the rest of the lunch hour just hanging out and talking about the animal shelter.

He said it was run by a really nice semi-retired couple who used to own a pet shop.

Then he took some photos out of his backpack and showed me all the animals that had already been placed in homes.

So, not only is Brandon a supertalented photographer, but he has a really BIG heart too.

And get this! We went to my locker to pick up my books, and then we walked to bio together!

SQUEEE!!!

MacKenzie kept glaring at me and whispering to Jessica the entire hour, but I just ignored her.

Okay, I admit it. I was wrong about the whole pity-invitation thing and Brandon not wanting to hang out with me.

I'm actually looking forward to going to his party.

And on Friday we're going to have a BLAST volunteering at Fuzzy Friends!!

Eat your heart out, MacKenzie!!
☺!!

THURSDAY, DECEMBER 5

During our library hour today Chloe and Zoey were busy making telephone calls trying to find a charity for the *Holiday on Ice* show.

Chloe called nine places and Zoey called seven, but no luck.

The deadline for entering is next week, and we're not even CLOSE to finding a charity.

But there's even MORE bad news!

I just found out today that MacKenzie is also planning to participate in the *Holiday on Ice* show ☹!!

Why am I NOT surprised?!

Probably because she really IS a coldhearted Ice Princess! Okay, so maybe that nasty little comment ISN'T quite true.

Her heart isn't COLD! She DOESN'T have one!!

MACKENZIE AS A HEARTLESS ICE PRINCESS

While I was at my locker, I overheard MacKenzie
bragging to some CCPs (Cute, Cool & Popular kids)

that she's been taking figure-skating lessons since she was seven years old and plans to skate to music from Swan Lake.

But this is the crazy part. She said she has FIVE charities BEGGING her to skate for them.

Can you believe THAT?! We're having trouble finding just one.

Although, now that I think about it, she was probably just saying all that stuff to impress everyone.

MacKenzie is SUCH a pathological liar! And a major DRAMA QUEEN.

I know it's supposed to be for a good cause. But I'm starting to get a really BAD feeling about this Holiday on Ice thing.

!

I could hardly wait for school to be over. Every class just seemed to drag on and on and on. After the final bell rang, I rushed to my locker and Brandon was already there waiting for me.

"Ready to go?" he said, smiling.

"Yep! Oh, wait! I have a present for you from Brianna," I said, digging into my backpack.

Brandon pretended to be frightened. "Brianna?! I don't know if I want it," he teased. "She says I have cooties. I don't think she likes me."

"She does. Well . . . actually, she doesn't!" I giggled. "But she wanted you to have this."

I handed Brandon about two metres of red satin ribbon, and he looked a little confused. Then he playfully tied it around his head.

"Oooh! Just the look I was going for!" he joked.
"Tell Brianna I plan to wear it every day."

BRANDON, TOTALLY CRACKING ME UP WITH
HIS WICKED SENSE OF HUMOUR

I laughed really hard. "It's not for you, silly. It's for the animals. Brianna said if we tie bows around their necks, they'll look like presents. And since everyone loves a present, they'll find new homes really fast."

"The kid's a genius! Why didn't I think of that?"

I was a nervous wreck as we walked the four blocks to the Fuzzy Friends building. But Brandon kept me laughing the entire time.

Three new puppies had come in, and each one needed to be photographed.

They were absolutely adorable and playfully nibbled on my fingers.

I cut the ribbon into three pieces and tied them around their necks.

"Have a seat on the rug and hold the first puppy in your lap," Brandon instructed. "Your sweater will be the perfect background for a close-up."

THE PUPPY AND I BOTH SMILE
FOR THE CAMERA!

We finished up in about forty-five minutes, and Brandon placed the last puppy back in the cage.

I was a little sad when I went over to say goodbye to them. I especially liked the smallest one, which had a little circle around one eye. He barked and wagged his tail at me as if to say, "Please, don't go!"

But it felt really good knowing I was doing something to help them all find a new home.

I was just about to leave when the smallest puppy pressed his nose against the cage door and it swung open.

"HEY!" I said, surprised. "How did you—"

But before I could finish my sentence, he quickly jumped into my lap, knocking me off balance.

The other two puppies scampered close behind and pounced.

"WHOA!" I yelled as I fell over backwards on the floor.

"Brandon! Help! The puppies got loose!" I giggled as they tickled my neck and chin.

But that guy was no help WHATSOEVER.

Not only was he LAUGHING at me, he just stood there taking pictures.

His camera sounded like he was at a photo shoot for Fashion Week or something. *Chick-koo. Chick-koo. Chick-koo. Chick-koo.*

"My bad!" he said, grinning. "I guess I closed the cage but didn't latch it. Smile and say 'CHEESE!'"

"Brandon! I'm going to . . . KILL you!" I laughed as I tried unsuccessfully to herd the wiggly puppies back into the cage.

We finished up and walked back to school. Then I called my mom to come pick me up.

While we were waiting, Brandon made a very special thank-you card for Brianna. . .

Those little pups looked SO SWEET in that photo!

I just knew Brianna was going to LOVE it!

And that red ribbon was perfect. I couldn't decide who wore it better, Brandon or the puppies.

Then Brandon totally surprised me and printed some of the snapshots he'd taken during the GREAT PUPPY ESCAPE. . .

I couldn't believe I had actually lost my balance and fallen over like that.

OMG! What if Brandon now thinks I'm just a big, clumsy . . . OX?! Or even worse, a big, clumsy . . . HAIRY-LEGGED, CRUSTY-EYED . . . ox?!

Okay, I really need to take a CHILL PILL and stop worrying about what he thinks of me.

Hanging out with Brandon at Fuzzy Friends wasn't like a real date or anything.

But I have to admit, I had the best time EVER!

☺!

SATURDAY, DECEMBER 7

It's hard to believe that the holidays are right around the corner.

Mom and I spent most of the morning decorating our fake Christmas tree.

Dad and Brianna were busy outside working on what they called a "super-duper secret project."

Dad said their big surprise was going to:

1. Spread holiday cheer.

2. Be a source of great pride for our family AND

3. Drastically INCREASE our household income.

But I was hoping he'd surprise us with something more practical.

Like a NEW JOB!

One that does NOT involve him:

1. Working at MY school.

2. Driving a crazy-looking van with a bug on it.

3. Exterminating bugs.

4. Damaging my already very shabby reputation.

Finally, Dad and Brianna called us outside to see their surprise.

I had a really BAD feeling about their little project even before I actually saw what they had done. Mostly because Dad and Brianna have the combined IQ of a TOOTHBRUSH.

And I was right!

I took one look at their monstrosity and totally

FREAKED. . .

I was like, WHAT is THAT?!

Riding around in Dad's van with that huge bug can be a pretty TRAUMATIC experience.

But undoing the psychological damage from Santa Roach, the Red-Nosed Christmas Tree is going to take years and years of intensive therapy.

I stared at Dad and Brianna in disbelief. "Please! Tell me this is all just a big PRANK?!"

That's when Brianna got this superserious look on her face and started speaking in this low, spooky voice.

"Nikki, you better be careful! Because on Christmas Eve, Santa Roach rises out of the pumpkin patch and gives out sweets and toys to all of the good little girls and boys! And he squirts bug spray into the eyes of all the BAD kids."

Which, by the way, is the MOST RIDICULOUS thing I've ever heard!!

Brianna must think I'm an IDIOT!! I know her little story is just a rip-off of another well-known legend.

But just in case any of that stuff she said about the bug spray is true, I'm going to start sleeping with my sunglasses on.

Anyway, this weekend I was seriously planning to come clean and tell Chloe and Zoey about my WCD scholarship and my dad being the school exterminator and all.

I'm just SO sick of all the deception and lies.

I had no doubt WHATSOEVER that Chloe and Zoey were my TRUE friends and would accept me for who I really am.

But that was BEFORE Santa Roach became a part of my STINKIN' family!!

There's just NO WAY I can tell my BFFs now!

☹!!

I was really surprised when I got up this morning and looked out the window. We had a really big snowstorm late last night and got, like, fifteen centimetres of snow.

My dad usually hates big snows. But today he was superexcited to go outside to clear the driveway.

Earlier in the year he bought this rusty old snowblower at a garage sale.

Dad is always buying dangerous pieces of junk from garage sales. I'll never forget the time he took us out on the lake in an old canoe with no paddles. If we hadn't been rescued by that coast guard helicopter, we probably would have drowned.

Dad insisted that he got a real bargain because a brand—new snowblower costs around $300 and he paid only $20 for his.

Well, now we all know why his snowblower was so

cheap. The snow-chute thingy was rusted and permanently stuck in one position. . .

DAD, TRYING TO CLEAR OUR DRIVEWAY WITH
HIS BROKEN SNOWBLOWER

That busted snowblower kept blowing snow right back on to the area Dad had just cleared. He couldn't figure out what he was doing wrong.

Poor Dad was out in the snow trying to clear the driveway for three hours. Mom had to go out there and drag him back into the house before his body parts froze solid.

I actually felt sorry for him. And Mom did too, because she went right online and ordered Dad a brand-new snowblower.

The bad news is that our driveway STILL needs to be dug out.

I explained to Mom I was willing to make a huge personal sacrifice and stay home from school for the next week or two until the new snowblower arrives.

But she just handed me a snow shovel and told me if I started shovelling right now, I'd have the driveway cleared out so I could go to school tomorrow morning.

Mom obviously had no appreciation for the
tremendous sacrifice I was willing to make.

Today in English, our teacher reminded us that our *Moby-Dick* report is due in nine days. We were supposed to start reading the novel back in October, but I've been very busy with other stuff.

It's about a humongous whale and this crusty old sailor who has a purse and a really bad attitude. I'm so NOT lying!

Like most people, I assumed that Moby Dick was the captain's name or something. But it was actually the whale's name. Like, WHO in their right mind would name a whale Moby Dick?!

Our report is supposed to be about why the captain and the whale were mortal enemies. But to save time, I'm thinking about just skipping the book and writing the paper.

Hey, you don't have to be a literary scholar (or read the book) to know WHY that whale was probably trying to kill that guy. . .

381

Hey, if my mom had named ME Moby Dick, I would have been massively ticked off about it too.

I think dusty old classics like these should come with a sticker on the cover that says:

WARNING

READING THIS BOOK CAN BE HAZARDOUS TO YOUR HEALTH!

WHY?! Because *Moby-Dick* was so ridiculously BORING, I accidentally fell asleep, smacked my head on my desk and darn near got a concussion!!

OMG! I had this big purplish bruise right in the middle of my forehead.

And I'd only got to the SECOND sentence!

As an additional precaution, I think students should be required to wear protective headgear while reading books like *Moby-Dick*.

Tomorrow I'm going to wear my bike helmet to class to protect against further head injuries.

BIKE HELMET

ME

Even though I was bummed about that paper being due next week, I was really looking forward to seeing Brandon today.

I wanted to tell him what a great time I had hanging out at Fuzzy Friends. And that I thought he'd make a great veterinarian one day.

But unfortunately, I didn't see him at lunch and he wasn't in bio.

It was the weirdest coincidence that while I was in the girls' toilets, I overheard Jessica and MacKenzie gossiping about Brandon.

Jessica said he had been called down to the office during first period and he'd left school for an important family matter. Well, that explained everything.

And get this! MacKenzie said it's rumoured that Brandon's dad is a wealthy U.S. diplomat at the French embassy and his mom is French royalty.

Apparently, his family lived in Paris for ten years, but he never talks about it because he probably wants to keep the fact that he's a prince or something a big secret. And that's why Brandon is fluent in French.

Then MacKenzie told Jessica that since she's an office assistant, she should check Brandon's school records to see if all those rumours are true.

But Jessica said she doesn't have access to certain information because it's kept on a special computer in the principal's office.

I was both shocked and appalled that those girls were actually talking about snooping in highly confidential student records.

It wasn't like I was eavesdropping on their very private conversation or anything. I was in that toilet cubicle totally minding my own business.

I just happened to feel like climbing up on the toilet seat, standing on my tippy toes and peeking over the top. To get, you know, some fresh air!

MACKENZIE AND JESSICA, GOSSIPING
ABOUT BRANDON

I just hope everything is okay with Brandon. I'm guessing he probably had a dentist appointment or something.

Jessica and MacKenzie are always sticking their noses in other people's business!

They are so PATHETIC!

But what if Brandon REALLY IS secretly a prince or something?!! He IS in Honours French!

OMG!!! SQUEEEEE!!

☺!!

TUESDAY, DECEMBER 10

I'm kind of in SHOCK right now ☹!!

Brandon just left my locker about thirty minutes ago. I could tell right away that something was really bothering him.

He gave me the rest of the photos he'd taken of me during the Great Puppy Escape and thanked me for helping him.

But when I mentioned how much fun I'd had and that I wanted to volunteer on a regular basis, he just looked really sad and stared at the floor.

Brandon explained that he'd just had some very bad news from Phil and Betty Smith, the owners of Fuzzy Friends. Phil broke his leg and is going to be in the hospital in traction for the next two months.

Unfortunately, there is no way Betty can keep the shelter open without his help.

BRANDON TELLS ME THE SAD NEWS
ABOUT FUZZY FRIENDS

As soon as Betty finds a place that will accept the eighteen cats and dogs in her shelter, she plans to sell the building to the flower shop next door.

No wonder Brandon was so upset. Starting tomorrow, he plans to spend every day after school helping to care for the animals until they all get transferred or placed in new homes.

I feel really bad for him. Mainly because I know how much he loves that place.

I mentioned all of this to Chloe and Zoey in gym class, and we had a deep discussion during sit-ups about how we could possibly help.

That's when I came up with the brilliant idea of Chloe, Zoey and me skating in the *Holiday on Ice* show to raise money for Fuzzy Friends!

Of course my BFFs were superhappy about us FINALLY finding a charity. They also said it's the perfect opportunity for ME to show Brandon what a good friend I am. Then Zoey said . . .

I just kind of smiled at Zoey and nodded.

But to be honest, I didn't have the slightest idea
WHAT she was talking about! Her comment had

NOTHING whatsoever to do with ANYTHING we were discussing!

Zoey is supersmart and I love her to death. But sometimes I wonder where she gets all of that cornball stuff.

Anyway, I agreed to discuss the *Holiday on Ice* idea with Brandon. We need a charity to skate for, and Fuzzy Friends needs the money to hire a part-time worker to replace Phil while he's recovering.

Zoey did the maths and calculated that the $3,000 donation from *Holiday on Ice* would probably be enough to pay a worker for about two months.

I just hope Brandon thinks all of this is a good idea.

I didn't want to mention it to Chloe and Zoey, but I'm really worried we might have a little competition for Fuzzy Friends from someone else.

While Brandon was talking to me at my locker, I

couldn't help but notice MacKenzie slinking around, pretending to be putting on lip gloss.

PUH-LEEZE! She could have put on twenty-seven layers of lip gloss during the time she was eavesdropping on our very private conversation.

That girl is a SNAKE and will stop at nothing to get what she wants.

I just hope she already has a charity, like she has been bragging to her CCP friends.

Because if she DOESN'T. . .?!

Things are going to get really UGLY!

☹!!

WEDNESDAY, DECEMBER 11

Right now I'm so MAD at MacKenzie I could just . . . SPIT!!

My suspicions were correct! According to the gossip around school, MacKenzie is skating for Fuzzy Friends!

YES! FUZZY FRIENDS!!! I was like, NO!! WAY!!

I can't believe MacKenzie is actually trying to steal MY charity from right under my nose like this. I came up with that idea first and she knows it. But I'm not going down without a fight!

When I saw her at her locker just now, she had the nerve to act all sweet and innocent. She even complimented my new sweater. Kind of.

She was all like, "Nikki! What a CUTE sweater! It's the PERFECT look! For a DOG. My poodle would LOVE it!"

MY SWEATER ☹

That girl is a charity-stealing BACKSTABBER!

I finally tracked Brandon down in the newspaper room during lunch. He had photos of all the animals at Fuzzy Friends and was busy typing up descriptions.

He explained that Betty is doubling her efforts to try to get all of her animals adopted before the shelter closes at the end of the month.

"OMG!" I exclaimed. "So soon?!"

I wanted to tell him about our plan to try to earn money for the shelter through the *Holiday on Ice* show.

But Brandon looked so down in the dumps. The last thing I wanted to do was set him up for another big disappointment.

Running that shelter was probably a lot of work. And it was very possible Betty just wanted to sell the building, collect the cash, retire to sunny Florida and play bingo every day for the rest of her life.

If she turned down our offer to help keep the shelter open, Brandon would just be more miserable than ever. I felt SO sorry for him.

"Is there anything I can do to help?" I asked.

Brandon looked up at me, and his face immediately brightened.

"Yeah, you can put these photos in order based on the ad numbers. Thanks! And no matter what happens, I just want you to know that I'll never forget you. . ." He nervously brushed his fringe out of his eyes and continued awkwardly. "Helping me with all of this stuff, I mean."

I was a little surprised he was so . . . serious. I tried to lighten the mood. "Hey, that's what friends are for. Even though YOU GOT COOTIES, DUDE!"

We both laughed really hard at my wacky impression of Brianna. Then we both kind of blushed and smiled at each other. All of this laughing, blushing and smiling went on, like, FOREVER.

Or at least, until we were RUDELY interrupted.

"Hello, people!" MacKenzie announced as she sashayed into the room. "Here I am!"

Then she dropped her Prada bag right on the stack of pictures I was sorting for Brandon.

BRANDON AND ME, GETTING RUDELY
INTERRUPTED

I rolled my eyes at MacKenzie while Brandon looked superannoyed.

Then she gave him a big fat phoney smile. "Brandon, I just had the most brilliant idea. You're going to be so thankful to me. But I need to talk to you about it ALONE!" she said in a breathy voice while batting her eyes like someone had thrown a fistful of sand in her face or something.

OMG! Watching that girl shamelessly flirt with Brandon like that was SO disgusting I actually threw up in my mouth a little.

Suddenly MacKenzie looked at me and scrunched up her nose like she smelled a funky foot odour. "Nikki, what are you doing in here? Don't you know this room is for experienced journalists only?"

"What I want to know is, WHY are YOU dressed like a tacky flight attendant?" I responded. "Are you here to write or to hand out peanuts?"

MACKENZIE AS A TACKY FLIGHT ATTENDANT

"PEANUTS FOR YOU. AND PEANUTS FOR YOU.
EVERYONE GETS SOME PEANUTS!!"

Brandon snickered but quickly covered it with a fake cough.

Hey! SHE started the fashion critiques with her doggie-sweater comment. I just finished it.

MacKenzie let out a high-pitched laugh, like she was in on the joke. But her eyes were shooting daggers at me.

"So, what are you working on today?" she asked Brandon, peering over his shoulder. Then she picked up a photo of a puppy.

"OMG! I LOVE puppies. Are they from that place called Fuzzy Friends? I heard they are closing down. I just hope those poor creatures won't be put to sleep. That'd be AWFUL! Hey, I have a great idea! Maybe I could help out by ska—"

Brandon's jaw tightened as he gritted his teeth. "Actually, MacKenzie, Nikki and I are working on a really important project. We're kind of busy right now. So if you don't mind, um. . ." He coughed again.

MacKenzie definitely got the hint.

403

"Oh! Well . . . I didn't mean to interrupt anything.
I just stopped by to get my, um. . ." She looked
around the room frantically until she spotted
something on the floor.

"My . . . PAPER CLIP!
Yep, it's right here.
I accidentally
dropped it on the
floor yesterday,
and I've been
looking everywhere
for it! Thank
goodness I found it!"

"I'm really happy for you,
MacKenzie," I said
sarcastically.

"Well, I guess I'll just talk to you later, Brandon.
When you're not so. . ." She shot me an evil look.
"BUSY. Goodbye!"

She plastered a fake smile across her face, winked

at Brandon and sashayed out of the room. I just HATE it when MacKenzie sashays.

It was quite obvious she had come to talk to Brandon about skating for Fuzzy Friends. And then she created all of that drama over a lost paper clip. How totally JUVENILE was that?!

Chloe, Zoey and I are planning to stop by the shelter on Saturday to talk to Betty, the owner. I just hope we get to her before MacKenzie does. I think MacKenzie is also CRAZY jealous that Brandon and I have been spending more time together lately.

But girlfriend needs to:

1. Cry a river.

2. Build a bridge AND

3. GET OVER IT!!

☺!!

THURSDAY, DECEMBER 12

AAAAAHHHHH! That is me SCREAMING.

WHY? I HATE taking those six-hour standardised tests for maths, science and reading comprehension!

You know, the one where your normally nice and friendly teacher suddenly turns into a MAXIMUM-SECURITY PRISON GUARD and marches around the room slapping the test booklet on your desk.

FORMERLY NICE TEACHER

SLAP!!

SLAP!!

Then, at the beginning of the test, she clicks this little stopwatch and yells. . .

"YOU MAY BEGIN . . . NOW!"

And at the end of the test, she clicks the little stopwatch again and yells. . .

"PLEASE STOP . . . NOW!"

Then she says, "Put DOWN your pencil! Do NOT turn the page. Put your HANDS above your HEAD. You have the right to remain silent. Anything you say can and will be used against you. You have the right to a lawyer. . ."

OMG! It's enough to scare the snot right out of you! No wonder students perform so poorly on these tests. But the worst part is that they compare your test scores with the scores of kids in your state and across the nation. This makes YOU look really BAD because the kids from those faraway schools are never as STUPID as the kids in your OWN school!

And since stupidity is more CONTAGIOUS than chicken pox, there is no way you can beat the test scores from those other schools.

Especially when you sit next to a seventeen-year-old guy who's STILL in eighth grade and STILL eats boogers.

So, under the circumstances, WHY would you even TRY to do well on the test when you already know your score is going to be LOUSY? I'm just sayin'!

That's why I'd like to see a CONNECT-THE-DOTS standardised test. Each student fills in those little circles on his/her answer sheet, and the test score is based on how CUTE and CREATIVE his/her picture is.

This type of testing would be more FAIR and, most important, a lot EASIER ☺!

I can't wait to score in the top 1% of the nation with all those smarty-pants AND earn an academic scholarship to Harvard University.

All because of my FABULOUS masterpiece!! . . .

BUTTERFLY BLISS IN #2 PENCIL

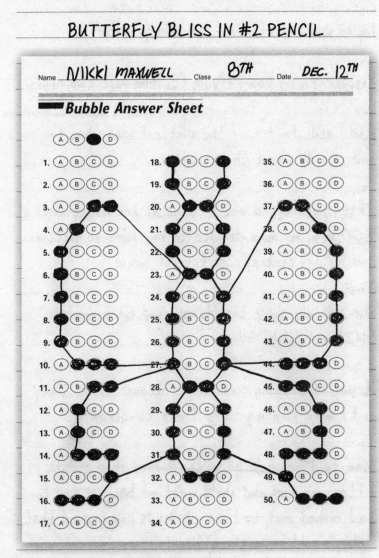

Am I not brilliant??!! ☺!!

FRIDAY, DECEMBER 13

I'm so upset right now I can barely write!

I've been in my room crying for the past two hours.

And I still don't have the slightest idea what I'm going to do about the situation.

After we dropped off Brianna at her ballet class at 5:00 p.m., my mom decided to buy some poinsettias and holiday centrepieces for our house.

She actually chose the flower shop right next to FUZZY FRIENDS!!

It was an amazing coincidence because Chloe, Zoey and I were planning to go there tomorrow.

Mom told me she'd be in the flower shop about fifteen minutes and she'd meet me back at the car. So I rushed over to Fuzzy Friends and prayed that Betty would be in the office.

Just inside the front door I saw a stack of empty moving boxes and my heart sank.

It looked like I was already too late!

I peeked inside a well-lit office and saw an older lady taking pictures off the walls.

"Excuse me! Are you Betty?" I asked.

"Yes, I am, dear. Come right in. This is the perfect time to adopt one of our pets, because we're going to be closing our doors really soon. Are you interested in a dog or cat?" She picked up a clipboard and gave me a big smile.

I immediately liked her.

And now I understand why Brandon likes her so much too.

"I'll need you to fill out a few forms. But the good news is that there's no charge at all!"

"Actually, I'm not here to adopt a pet. Although they're quite adorable. I was here last week as a student volunteer. And now I'm wondering if we could represent Fuzzy Friends in a school-related community service project?"

Betty motioned for me to sit down.

"Well, first of all, thank you for volunteering!" she said. "It's the wonderful and caring people like you who have allowed us to place more than two hundred animals so far this year. But unfortunately, a few days ago my husband fell off a ladder while painting the kitchen and broke his leg in two places. There's just no way we can continue to stay open."

I didn't waste any time and immediately explained the *Holiday on Ice* programme and how the money we earned could be used to help keep the centre open for a few months. Hopefully, until her husband fully recovered.

Betty became overwhelmed with emotion and suddenly burst into tears. . .

I wasn't the least bit surprised to hear what she said next.

"You know what?! Now that I think about it, I got a telephone message yesterday from a young lady about _Holiday on Ice._ But I assumed she was selling tickets. I think her name was Madison. Or was it Mikaya—"

"MACKENZIE?"

"Yes! That's it. MacKenzie! How did you know?"

"Oh! Just a lucky guess."

"Well, Nikki! Tell me how I can sign up Fuzzy Friends as a *Holiday on Ice* charity! I'm really looking forward to seeing you and your friends skate."

Our meeting went even better than I could have imagined.

She gave me her business card with her home telephone number and even the hospital number so I could reach her pretty much 24-7.

"Nikki, you have no idea how much this means to me, my husband and especially our grandson," Betty gushed. "Poor little guy! He's already been through so much, losing his parents a few years ago. And now we were going to have to uproot him and move to a new state in the middle of the year. I was dreading having to break the news to him, but thanks to you, I won't have to. He's out back exercising the dogs. All I can say is thank you, thank you!" Then she hugged me so hard, I could barely breathe.

"Thank YOU! For agreeing to be our charity and allowing us to skate for you," I said, tearing up a little myself. "We'll try to make Fuzzy Friends proud!"

As I left the shelter I noticed a tall fence that surrounded the entire property.

I heard what sounded like a pack of dogs barking excitedly and couldn't help but sneak a peek.

I saw a boy running around with what appeared to be eight dogs of assorted sizes, colours and breeds, including the three puppies.

Even though his back was to me, I could see the boy had one of those soft foam rubber footballs and seemed to be having a rousing football game of guy versus dogs. . .

He ran with the football across the grass, dodging imaginary tackles, as the dogs happily chased after him, barking and nipping at his heels.

"And it's a TOUCHDOWN!!" he screamed. "And the CROWD GOES WILD!! HAAAAAARRR!"

That's when I noticed his voice sounded vaguely familiar.

But my brain refused to make the connection and instead decided he must just sound like someone I knew.

The boy spiked the football into the ground and broke into a funky chicken/running man inspired victory dance as the dogs barked and ran in frenzied circles around him.

Then he and all the dogs collapsed on the ground in sheer exhaustion.

When I finally saw his face, I froze and gasped in shock. . .

IT WAS BRANDON!!

Suddenly that comment he made a couple days ago, about never forgetting me no matter what happened, took on a whole new meaning.

He KNEW that IF Fuzzy Friends closed, there was a chance he and his grandparents might be moving away during the holiday break!

NOOO! THIS CAN'T BE HAPPENING!! OMG! OMG! OMG!

Brandon and I might not EVER see each other AGAIN! ☹!!

SATURDAY, DECEMBER 14

The shock about Brandon is finally starting to wear off a little.

But I still have a million questions:

WHO is Brandon, really?

WHERE is he from?

WHAT happened to his parents?

WHEN did he start living with his grandparents?

HOW did he end up at WCD?

And what about all that stuff I overheard MacKenzie and Jessica saying about Brandon in the toilets?! Is any of that true?

Just thinking about all this is enough to make my head spin and my heart hurt.

I can't begin to imagine what he's gone through.

But I don't dare breathe a word of this to another living soul. Not even Chloe and Zoey.

If Brandon wants anyone to know, he can tell them.

Well, at least something good happened today. I mailed off the paperwork, so now it's official!

Chloe, Zoey and I will be skating in the *Holiday on Ice* show for the charity Fuzzy Friends!

And I plan to do everything within my power to help keep that place open.

For the animals.

For Betty and Phil.

And most important, for . . . BRANDON!

I <u>KNOW</u> I CAN DO THIS. ☺!!

ARRRGH!!

I'm so ticked off at Brianna and Miss Penelope right now, I could just . . . SCREAM!!

But since this whole thing was Mom's STUPID idea, it's technically all HER fault!

You'd think that after giving birth to two children, she would be a more responsible parent!

Why in the world would she ask ME to take over the family tradition of baking holiday cookies for friends and neighbours?!

I should have suspected that something was up when Mom started acting really weird at dinner.

After setting the table, she just stood there, like a mannequin or something, holding on to my chair and staring at me with this strange look on her face.

But since I was pretty much starving, I just ignored her and continued to stuff my face.

Suddenly Mom's eyes glazed over and she stopped blinking. This could mean only one thing.

She'd somehow suffered a head injury while making dinner and needed emergency medical care. Or maybe NOT.

"Mom! Are you okay?!" I said through a mouthful of food.

"Oh!" She suddenly snapped out of her daze as a big sappy grin spread across her face. "I was just thinking about how wonderful it would be to pass my cookie tradition on to YOU, so that one day you can share it with YOUR daughter."

"HUH?!" I gasped, almost choking on my mashed potatoes.

WHY were we talking about BABIES?!

Brandon and I HADN'T even held hands yet!

I was happy Mom had such pleasant memories of

baking cookies with me when I was a little kid. . .

MOM →

SHE'S SO CUTE!

ME
↓

MOM AND ME (AT AGE FIVE),
BAKING HOLIDAY COOKIES

<u>Sorry!</u> But I was so NOT looking forward to baking cookies with my OWN daughter.

<u>Mainly</u> because I had this fear she would be a little TERROR as punishment for all the HEADACHES I had caused my mom. . .

ME AND MY DAUGHTER (AT AGE FIVE),
BAKING HOLIDAY COOKIES

That's when Mom placed her hands on my shoulders and looked into my eyes.

"Nikki, will you make the Christmas cookies this year?! It would mean so very much to me."

My gut reaction was to scream, "Mom, stop it! You're SCARING me!"

But instead I just shrugged, swallowed a forkfull of mashed potato, and muttered, "Um . . . okay."

I mean, how hard could baking cookies be? Moms do it all the time. Right?!

After dinner was over, Mom handed me the cookie recipe so I could get started. Then she headed for the mall to finish up her Christmas shopping.

The thing that bothered me most was that Mom had very conveniently left out an important detail. I had to bake cookies with BRIANNA. ☹!!

I tried to cook a gourmet dinner with Brianna back in September and it was a total disaster.

And I was STILL haunted by the horrible memory of making homemade ice cream at Thanksgiving and both Brianna and Dad getting their tongues stuck on the metal ice-cream thingy!

427

Brianna came skipping into the kitchen.

"Hi, Nikki! Guess what? Me and Miss Penelope are here to help you bake cookies!"

I was like, JUST GREAT ☹!!

I knew I had to keep Brianna really busy so she wouldn't get in my way or do something predictably dangerous.

Like, stuff Miss Penelope in the microwave on the popcorn setting to see if she would magically turn into a bucket of popcorn.

So to distract Brianna, I asked her to go find me two cookie sheets.

Things got off to a great start. I had measured all the ingredients and was about to start mixing.

That's when Brianna started making so much noise, it sounded like a construction work site.

CLANK! BANG! KLUNK! CLANK!

"Brianna, I can barely hear myself think! Stop making all that noise before you make my head explode!" I yelled.

Her eyes lit up. "Really? This noise will make your head explode? COOL!"

CLANK! BANG! KLUNK!

"Brianna! Knock it off! Or I'm calling Mom. . . !" I threatened.

"Look at me!" she said, doing the robot around the kitchen. "I'm the Tin Man from *The Wizard of Oz*!"

"Sorry, Brianna! You're NOT the Tin Man," I muttered. "You need a BRAIN! THAT would make you the SCARECROW!"

"Nikki! I do got a BRAIN!" she huffed. "SEE?" She opened her mouth really wide and pointed.

I pulled out a chair from the kitchen table and set it in front of her.

"Just sit here and don't move, like a good little Tin Man. Just pretend you're rusting or something. Okay?"

I mixed the cookie ingredients together, rolled out the dough and made little Christmas trees with Mom's cookie cutters.

Then I placed the cookies in the oven. When I turned around, Brianna was licking the spoon.

"Brianna, don't lick the spoon! I need to use it to make this last batch of cookies."

"It's Miss Penelope's fault, not mine. She's tasting the cookie dough to make sure it's not nasty. She says you're really good at drawing, but your cooking STINKS!"

I could NOT believe Miss Penelope was talking trash about me like that. Especially since she wasn't even a real . . . um . . . HUMAN.

I thought about grabbing the rolling pin and giving Miss Penelope something really nasty to "taste".

But instead I decided to chillax by watching TV in the family room while my cookies baked for thirteen minutes.

It hadn't been more than five minutes when I thought I smelled something burning.

I rushed back into the kitchen, and Brianna was standing near the stove with this really guilty look on her face.

The oven temperature had been changed from 350 degrees to, like, a thousand! This is what happened. . .

I told Miss Penelope NOT to turn the oven on high. But she wanted the cookies to get done fast 'cause she's really HUNGRY!

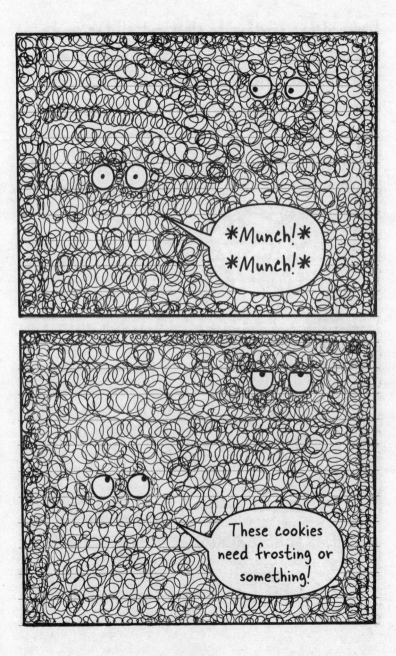

435

I opened the windows to clear out all the smoke and hoped the fire department wouldn't show up. OMG! I'll just DIE if my face ends up plastered on the front page of the city newspaper!

75¢

WESTCHESTER NEWS

MONDAY DEC. 16

Baking Fiasco!

Holiday Tradition Goes up in SMOKE!

NO COOKIES THIS YEAR!

TEEN FAILS
By Verr E. Embarrassing

ME, PLASTERED ACROSS THE FRONT PAGE

This little baking project was a complete and utter DISASTER!

Now I have to call Mom and break the news that she needs to stop by the supermarket on her way home from the mall.

Because this year, thanks to Brianna and Miss Penelope, all our friends and family members will be receiving holiday cookies baked in a hollow tree by those little Keebler Elves! I'm just sayin'. . . ☹!!

I can't believe that we actually start ice skating in gym class tomorrow. Soon I'll be gliding across the ice and doing double-axel jumps like the pros.

I plan to go to bed an hour early tonight so I'll be alert and well rested.

It's going to be weird hanging around Brandon now that I know his situation. I'm still really worried about him.

But I think I'm starting to like him even MORE! ☺!!

Right now I'm SO frustrated I could just . . .

SCREAM ☹!!

Today was my first day of ice skating at the high school arena during gym class, and it was a complete DISASTER!

Just standing up on the ice was, like, ten times harder than I thought it was going to be.

WHY, WHY, WHY did I ever agree to do this stupid *Holiday on Ice* show?!

I must have been temporarily INSANE.

And it didn't help matters that MacKenzie was FUMING over the fact that Chloe, Zoey and I were skating for Fuzzy Friends, and not HER.

As usual, that girl went out of her way to make my life MISERABLE. . .

I can't believe MacKenzie actually said that right to my face like that.

The entire class heard it too. It seemed like everyone was snickering about me behind my back.

OMG! I was beyond HUMILIATED!

We were SUPPOSED to be practising our *Holiday on Ice* skating routine during gym class.

But *NOOOO*! I didn't practise at all. WHY?!!

BECAUSE I'M SO HORRIBLY CRUDDY AT ICE SKATING, I COULDN'T EVEN STAND UP! THAT'S WHY!!

Chloe and Zoey even held both my hands like I was a clumsy little toddler taking my first steps. But I *STILL* fell down!

The ONLY thing I could do really well was a move that required superwobbly legs.

Well, I'm really sorry to disappoint those snobby CCPs! But any dance I was doing was PURELY accidental.

Chloe and Zoey told me to chillax and be patient because it might take three or four weeks of practising before I could even skate around the rink by myself.

But our ice show is in only TWO WEEKS!! Girlfriends, do the MATHS!!

Zoey suggested that I read her book *Figure Skating for Dummies*.

And Chloe offered to loan me her novel *The Ice Princess*.

But personally, I don't think books are going to help me much.

The only TWO things I really NEED right now are:

One of those walker thingies that really old people

use, because six legs on the ice are better than just two. . .

And a really soft pillow because I now have a dozen bruises from falling on my behind, and I'm NOT going to be able to sit down for a week. . .

Unfortunately, we'll be practising our ice-skating
routine in gym class for the rest of the week.

And then on December 26, 27 and 30, we have three
special practice sessions for the December 31 show.

444

I don't mean to be all doom-'n'-gloom, but this ice-skating stuff is turning into a total NIGHTMARE!

AAAAAAHHHHHH!!!!

That was me screaming in frustration. AGAIN!

But I have to remain calm and stay focussed.

I can't afford to fail. Because if I do, Brandon will be forced to move, and he's had enough trauma in his life.

OMG! WHAT have I got myself into??!

☹!!

I'm sitting in my bedroom trying not to have a TOTAL MELTDOWN.

I just HATE it when I do things at the very last minute.

My *Moby-Dick* assignment is due in less than fourteen hours and I'm just now starting it.

By "it" I don't mean the book REPORT.

I'm just starting to READ the stupid BOOK ☹!!

My biggest fear is that the book might aggravate a very serious medical problem.

You see, I'm superALLERGIC to . . . BORING!

There's a possibility that while I'm reading *Moby-Dick*, I could have a SEVERE allergic reaction due to extreme BOREDOM and go into anaphylactic shock.

I could, like, actually . . . DIE!!

MY PAINFUL AND SENSELESS DEATH
FROM SEVERE BOREDOM DUE TO READING
MOBY-DICK

Then my teacher would give me a big fat
INCOMPLETE for my grade because I didn't finish
the assignment!

OMG! What if she made me attend SUMMER

SCHOOL to make up for the incomplete?! How CRUDDY would THAT be?!

Thank goodness I'd already be DEAD due to my allergic reaction to boredom ☺!!

Anyway, I had no idea how I was going to read the entire 672-page book AND write a report. But I was DETERMINED to do it.

So I pulled out my *Moby-Dick* book and started reading as fast as my little eyeballs could go.

The good news was that if I read six pages a minute, I could finish the book in less than two hours ☺!!

I was pleasantly surprised when I didn't immediately doze off or have any major medical complications from my boredom allergy.

But after what seemed like forever, I was so mentally exhausted, the words were just a blur on the page. That's when I decided to stop and take a short fifteen-minute break from my intensive reading.

Especially since, according to my clock, I'd been reading for an entire seven minutes AND had blazed my way through three whole pages.

After quickly recalculating my numbers, I made a very shocking and grim discovery.

At the rate I was currently working, it was going to take me FOREVER to read the book, assuming I DIDN'T stop to rest, eat, get a drink of water, sleep, or go to the toilet.

I was so NOT happy about this situation.

That's when I suddenly got this overwhelming urge to rip the pages out of that book one by one and flush them down the TOILET while hopping on one foot.

DON'T ASK! I was suffering from mental exhaustion.

How BADLY did I NOT want to read *Moby-Dick*?

I actually made a list. . .

5 THINGS I'D RATHER DO THAN READ *MOBY-DICK*

1. Pluck out my eye with a dirty spatula
2. Clean every toilet in the house with a toothbrush
3. Brush my teeth with the toothbrush I used to clean every toilet in the house
4. Visit our neighbour lady, Mrs Wallabanger, for a detailed update on her bunion surgery
5. Hang out with Brianna

HANG OUT WITH BRIANNA?!

I could NOT believe I actually wrote those words.

Especially after she totally grossed me out at dinner tonight.

HOW?

By opening her mouth to show me her partially chewed broccoli tuna casserole.

While Hawaiian Punch dribbled out of her nose.

OMG! It was all so NASTY I couldn't even finish my meal!

It's making me queasy again just thinking about it.

Finally, I'd had enough. I slammed my *Moby-Dick* book shut and threw it across the room in utter frustration.

Then I walked down the hall and stuck my head inside Brianna's room.

"Hey, Brianna! What's up?"

She was sprawled on the floor playing dolls.

"The Wicked Witch has thrown Princess Sugar Plum into the ocean, and Baby Unicorn is trying to rescue her. But since he can't swim, the Magic Baby Dolphin has to help," Brianna explained.

"Sounds fun!" I said.

"Do you wanna play too?" Brianna asked excitedly.

"Sure!" I said, and flopped down on the floor next to her.

Okay, what was more important?

Spending quality time with my wonderful little sister?

Or reading *Moby-Dick*?

Mom would have been proud!

Brianna picked up her Magic Baby Dolphin and changed her voice to a high squeak. "Hurry, Baby

Unicorn! Jump into My Designer Dream Boat and we'll go rescue Princess Sugar Plum."

I placed Baby Unicorn on the boat and did my best impression of Alvin from *Alvin and the Chipmunks.* "Okay, let's go! Thank you, Magic Baby Dolphin, for helping me! How will I ever repay you?"

"You can come to my birthday party and bring lots of sweets! I'm going to have a pizza party at Queasy Cheesy. With chocolate cake, too," Brianna said happily.

"Oooh! Goody gumdrops! I just LOVE Queasy Cheesy! And chocolate cake," ~~I said~~ Baby Unicorn said.

"Just keep an eye out for sharks!" Magic Baby Dolphin added. "They have very pointy teeth, you know!"

"AAAHHH! SHARKS! Get me outta here!!" Baby Unicorn screamed as she ran and hid.

"Wait! Come back, Baby Unicorn! Who's going to

save Princess Sugar Plum?!" Magic Baby Dolphin cried.

"I dunno! Call 911! Sharks have very pointy teeth. And I'm allergic to very pointy teeth!" Baby Unicorn screamed hysterically.

Brianna giggled. "Nikki! This is just like the Princess Sugar Plum MOVIE! Only, more FUN!"

That's when a little lightbulb popped on in my brain. BOAT?! FISH?! POINTY TEETH?! MOVIE?!

"Brianna! I have an idea! Let's shoot a real movie! You go run water in the bathtub, and I'll get Dad's video camera. This is going to be a blast!"

Brianna squealed with excitement. "YAY! I'm gonna go put on my Princess Sugar Plum swimsuit."

I ran back to my room and read over my *Moby-Dick* assignment sheet.

It said, "Please focus on two central themes — the allegorical significance of the whale, Moby Dick, and the deceptiveness of fate. Your report can be written or presented in any other suitable format. BE CREATIVE!"

This was GREAT news! I quickly skimmed the last few pages of *Moby-Dick*.

I felt kind of sorry for that Captain Ahab guy. In the end he was so wrapped up in his quest for revenge that he went completely overboard in his final attempt to kill that whale. No pun intended!

I quickly gathered some props. Then I auditioned my actors and cast the parts.

Of course Brianna wanted to be the STAR of the movie. And since none of those teen actors from the Disney and Nickelodeon channels were available at such short notice, I finally gave in and let her do it.

MOBY-DICK — CAST OF CHARACTERS

ISHMAEL, narrator and member of *Pequod* whaling ship crew

(Played by Kent fashion doll)

CAPTAIN AHAB, crazy captain of the *Pequod*. Totally obsessed with killing the whale, Moby Dick, after it bit off his leg.

(Played by Wicked Witch of the West doll)

THE *PEQOUD*, a very dreary whaling ship sailing on the Atlantic Ocean

(Played by My Designer Dream Boat)

MOBY DICK, the killer White Whale

(Played by Brianna Maxwell)

Shooting our movie was pretty challenging. To create the stormy ocean, I decided to use a fan.

OKAY! LIGHTS, CAMERA, ACTION!

ROAR!!

We finished filming in about an hour. I think my movie turned out pretty well. Especially considering the fact that I had a cast of inexperienced actors, no budget and it wasn't shot on location.

I just hope I get a decent grade.

But most importantly, I learned a very crucial lesson about the dangers of procrastination. . .

NEVER, EVER wait until the last minute to do a major homework assignment!

UNLESS, of course, your little sister can do a really good killer whale impersonation! ROAR!!

I'm thinking about entering my video in one of those prestigious Hollywood film festivals.

Who knows?! Maybe one day *Moby Dick Battles Princess Sugar Plum on My Designer Dream Boat* will be playing at a cinema near you.

☺!!

WEDNESDAY, DECEMBER 18

OMG ☹!!

I have never been so HUMILIATED in my entire life!

Today in gym our teacher announced that we were going to spend the entire hour watching a very special group of skaters perform.

She said they were talented, hardworking and deserved our utmost respect and admiration.

Next she explained that she would be scoring the skaters while the class watched.

I was so happy and relieved to hear this news that I actually did a Snoopy "happy dance" inside my head.

I'm just really bad at ice skating. And instead of improving, I swear it seems like I'm getting WORSE.

I was looking forward to seeing those supertalented

high school kids skate. Maybe I could even learn a thing or two.

Then things got REALLY weird.

Our teacher asked MacKenzie, Chloe, Zoey and me to stand.

Then she announced that each one of us was going to individually perform the skating routine that we were working on for the *Holiday on Ice* show.

Of course MacKenzie, Chloe and Zoey were more than happy to show off their skills on the ice.

ME? I almost PEED my pants! Every cell in my body wanted to run out of there SCREAMING. But instead, I just shrugged and said, "Um . . . okay."

Even though MacKenzie still hadn't found a charity sponsor, her routine was sheer perfection.

On ice, she was like a graceful fairy snow princess or something. . .

462

463

When MacKenzie finished her routine, she got
a standing ovation from the class. And our gym
teacher gave her a fantastic score of 9.5! I was
practically green with envy.

I was up next. As I stepped onto the ice I gave
myself a little pep talk. I CAN DO THIS! I CAN
DO THIS! I CAN DO THIS! I CAN DO THIS!

I ended my routine by tripping over my feet and sliding across the ice on my stomach like a HUMAN PUCK.

And just when I thought my skating routine couldn't get any worse, I slammed into a hockey net and it fell over, trapping me inside . . .

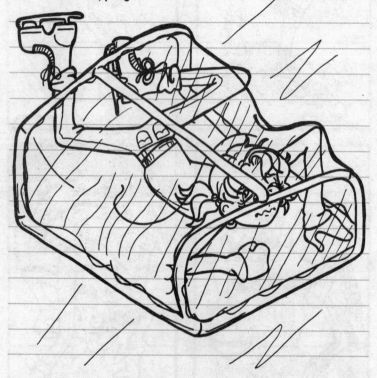

. . . like some kind of giant LOBSTER CREATURE in lip gloss, hoop earrings and ice skates.

Of course all of the jocks jumped up and yelled, "GOAL!!" and gave each other high fives.

It seemed like the entire class was pointing and laughing at me. I wanted to cry really, really badly! I didn't know which hurt more, my gut or my ego.

Then, to add insult to injury, I saw my score. . .

I could NOT believe my gym teacher had actually given me a NEGATIVE FOUR!

Hey, I'm NOT a professional judge or anything. But any IDIOT knows there are no NEGATIVE numbers in figure skating!

I was SO mad! I actually told off my teacher right in front of the entire class.

"Listen, sister! Let me see YOU get YOUR DUSTY BUTT out there on the ice and NOT BREAK A HIP or something!!"

But I just said that inside my head, so no one else heard it but me.

Chloe and Zoey rushed over to help me up and asked if I was okay.

I told them I was just fine, thank you! Then I went straight to the girls' locker room and started writing in my diary.

I'm sure Chloe and Zoey will each do really well on their routines.

Then they'll get a standing ovation from our class and a superhigh score from our teacher, just like MacKenzie!

That's because all three of them are really talented skaters.

Unlike ME!!

But I'm not jealous of them or anything.

I mean, how JUVENILE would THAT be?!!

SORRY! But I CAN'T DO THIS ANYMORE!!

I QUIT!!
☹!!

THURSDAY, DECEMBER 19

I felt really horrible giving up when so much was at stake for Brandon and his family.

But the show was only eleven days away. There was just no way I was going to be able to improve enough to NOT make a complete FOOL out of myself.

The director of the ice show is Victoria Steel, a famous Olympic gold medalist figure skater.

I heard from Chloe that she's superstrict. She yells at skaters when they fall, even though it's just a charity event. And last year she actually cut a skater from a show because she said the girl was an embarrassment!

If I stayed on the team for Fuzzy Friends, there was a risk we could get cut from the show and lose the $3,000 needed to keep the shelter open.

I couldn't take that chance.

As of yesterday, MacKenzie STILL needed a charity. So the mature and responsible thing to do was to ~~ask~~ BEG her to take my place and skate for Fuzzy Friends.

I really didn't have a choice in the matter.

This was the ONLY way I could help Brandon.

And YES! I felt AWFUL!

My biggest fear was that he was going to think I was an immature, undisciplined, untalented, ungraceful, self-centred BRAT!

I planned to explain everything to him tomorrow and then break the news to Chloe and Zoey.

But Brandon showed up today while I was working in the library.

Chloe and Zoey had just left to pick up several boxes of new library books from the office, and I was the only person at the front desk.

ME, NOT NOTICING BRANDON STANDING
THERE WATCHING ME WRITE IN MY DIARY

"Hey, Nikki!"

"OMG! Brandon? Hi! I didn't see you standing there!"

"So, how's the skating coming?"

"Actually, I wanted to talk to you about that. There's something I need to tell you. And I was hoping you could give Betty the message."

"Oh, really!" Brandon said, smiling. "That's funny, because I have a message from HER to YOU."

"You do? Well, you can go first," I said.

"I'm not in a big hurry. You can go first."

"No! YOU!"

I looked at him and he looked at me.

"OKAY! I'll go!" we both said at the same time.

Then we laughed.

"I give up, Maxwell. You win! I'll go first. . ."
Brandon chuckled.

Then he reached down and grabbed a bag.

"Betty asked me to give this to you. She said she wouldn't be able to keep the shelter open without your help, and it's just a small token of her appreciation."

Brandon brushed his fringe out of his eyes and gave me a big smile.

I just stared at the bag and then Brandon and then the bag and then Brandon again.

"Well?" Brandon said, still holding it out to me. "Why don't you open it? I'm supposed to make sure you like it."

As I accepted the bag from him, a big dopey smile spread across my face and I blushed profusely.

Although I was smiling on the outside, I was a complete emotional wreck on the inside.

How was I supposed to tell Brandon I was quitting the ice show when Betty had just sent me what appeared to be a thankyou gift?

Inside the bag was a small, thin gift-wrapped box. The wrapping paper had pictures of the cutest puppies wearing red bows. Just like our Great Puppy Escape photos.

But then I took a closer look. It WAS our photos! Brandon had printed them up as gift wrap.

"AWWWWW!! How cute!" I gushed.

I tore open the wrapping paper and inside was a DVD of the Disney movie *Lady and the Tramp*.

"OMG, Brandon! This was my favourite when I was a little kid! It's PERFECT!"

Brandon smiled. "I was hoping you'd like it!"

"I DO! And Brianna's going to love it too!"

Brandon crossed his arms, leaned against the desk and stared right at me.

"So . . . what was it you wanted to tell ME?" he asked.

JUST GREAT ☹!! Right then I felt like a total JERK!

"Well, I – I just was . . . um. . ." I stammered.

WHO would quit on a poor lady struggling with an orphaned grandson, a sick husband and eighteen homeless animals AFTER she'd just sent a wonderful thankyou present?

Only a coldhearted SNAKE, that's who!

"Actually, it's kind of about MacKenzie."

I hesitated, staring nervously at the floor.

"She's an excellent skater, and I was thinking she—"

"Listen, Nikki. Don't worry about MacKenzie! She's been hanging around trying to get Betty to change her mind. But Betty is sticking with you, Chloe and Zoey. Besides, in bio today I overheard MacKenzie telling Jessica she was going to be skating for a fashion school or something."

I was shocked to hear that MacKenzie had finally found a sponsor.

"A fashion school? Are you kidding?" I exclaimed. "Wait, don't tell me. . ."

I put my hand on my hip and did my best MacKenzie impression.

"Hon! Like, my very fabulous charity is from the Westchester Institute of Fashion and Cosmetology. Which, by the way, is owned by my aunt Clarissa!"

Brandon looked amused. "Yeah, actually, I think that's EXACTLY what she said. It's owned by her aunt . . . Clarissa?"

"Yeah, I bet MacKenzie convinced her aunt to start a new charity to make our city more beautiful. She stands on street corners handing out designer clothing to the fashionably challenged!" I joked.

That girl is so INCREDIBLY vain. . .

MACKENZIE, MAKING OUR CITY MORE BEAUTIFUL!

Thanks to her aunt Clarissa, MacKenzie was now completely OUT of the picture. Which meant ME and my very bruised behind were back IN.

I needed to go to my Emergency Plan B. Only I didn't have one.

Brandon folded his arms. "So, what is it I'm supposed to tell Betty?" he asked again.

"Actually, Brandon, just tell her I LOVE the DVD. And thanks!"

"Thank YOU!" Brandon said softly as his eyes locked on to mine.

OMG! Talk about major RCS.

My knees felt all weak and wobbly, and I wasn't even on the ice.

Brandon glanced at his watch. "Uh-oh! I better get back to class."

He gave me another one of his crooked smiles and I tried not to swoon. Very much.

After Brandon left, I collapsed into my chair.

This was BAD!

Very, very BAD!!

But when I picked up my new *Lady and the Tramp* DVD, for some reason I started to feel better.

Probably because my very favourite scene was on the cover. You know the one.

The famous SPAGHETTI KISS!

That's when I started to wonder if Brandon likes spaghetti.

What if on our very first date we went to a quaint little Italian restaurant and shared a plate of spaghetti? We'd get. . .

SQUEEE ☺!!

Hey! It could actually happen!! Hmmm . . . I wonder how much private lessons with a figure skating coach cost . . . ?

ME, AS A GRACEFUL ICE PRINCESS TRAINING WITH MY COACH!

FRIDAY, DECEMBER 20

Today is the last day of school! This means I'm officially on winter break! WOO-HOO ☺!

Christmas is my most favourite holiday! WHY?!

Because you get lots of presents AND a long break from school! It's like having a birthday and a mini summer holiday all rolled into one.

How cool is THAT?!

The only downside is that by the time you hit middle school, most parents really start slacking off on their gift-giving responsibilities.

Every year I get the same old cruddy gifts. Pyjamas, socks, fruitcake, and an electric toothbrush with no batteries in it (DUH!).

I'm so DISGUSTED! I have such a large inventory of cheap, junky gifts I could actually open my own DOLLAR STORE or something. . .

But THIS year is going to be different! And yes, it was probably a little tacky of me to "accidentally" leave copies of my wish list plastered all over the house for Mom to find. . .

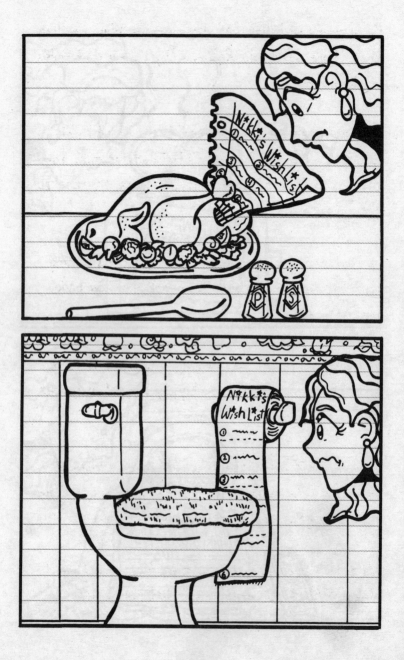

I'm sure my wish list was way more exciting reading than those dusty old *Reader's Digests* my dad keeps in the bathroom.

Anyway, when Mom announced that she had not just ONE, but TWO early Christmas presents for Brianna and me to open — I was pleasantly shocked and surprised.

Had I known my brilliant, in-your-face marketing strategy was going to work so well, I would have used it years ago.

The larger present was SO big, I guessed that it probably contained my new laptop computer, mobile phone, art supplies AND cash.

"I hope it's a chocolate cake!" Brianna screamed excitedly. "I'm going to have a Princess Sugar Plum chocolate cake for my birthday!"

We both ripped open our gift at the same time. I almost FAINTED when I saw what was inside. . .

"MOM!! WHAT THE. . .?!!
A PRINCESS SUGAR PLUM DRESS?!"

Apparently, Mom had paid our neighbour lady,
Mrs Wallabanger, to make us these sickeningly

frilly MATCHING Princess Sugar Plum dresses.

Then Mom got all emotional and teary-eyed.

"Girls, the best part is that tomorrow you'll be wearing these beautiful dresses to a VERY special event!"

I was like, "Mom! Are you KA-RAY-ZEE??!!"

But I just said that inside my head, so no one else heard it but me.

I hoped that the event was going to be at a junkyard, an abandoned parking garage, a cow pasture, or a sewage treatment plant. Anywhere there'd be a limited number of life-forms to see me in that UGLY dress!

Mom giggled and begged us to open our second present. Judging from the very small size, I was hoping it was a box of matches.

Then I'd be able to BURN my new dress in the fireplace. But no such luck ☹!

"SURPRISE!! For Family Sharing Time, we're going to see the *Nutcracker* ballet!" Mom exclaimed.

I was SO frustrated I wanted to scream!

"AAAAAHHHHH!"

WHY was my mom giving me an UGLY dress and a BORING ballet theater ticket, when I've been BEGGING for a new PHONE for, like, FOREVER?!

Had she not even BOTHERED to READ the twenty-seven copies of my wish list that I had discreetly left lying around the house?!

Hey, if I'm gonna watch a stage show, it better include slammin' vocals, krazy-good dancers, special effects, fireworks, loud guitar solos and crowd surfing.

I am so NOT looking forward to this.

If Mom really wants to TORTURE me, she should just make me stay home and BABYSIT BRIANNA while blasting Dad's LAME disco music until my EARS BLEED.

I'm just saying . . .

!!

I just stared at myself in the mirror in total disbelief.

How was this possible?

I HATED that hideous dress even MORE than I did yesterday.

I decided it was time to take legal action. I was going to sue my parents.

For CRUELTY to children!

"Girls! It's time to go!" Mom chirped cheerfully. "I can't wait to see how beautiful the two of you look!"

I adjusted the huge bow in my hair, which was the size of a small seagull.

I looked just like one of those creepy Victorian porcelain dolls you find in antique shops.

ME, AS A VERY
CREEPY VICTORIAN
PORCELAIN DOLL

To make matters
worse, the fancy
shoes were killing
my feet. I so
wanted to wear
my worn-out
converse.

It was going to
be painful enough
to have to sit
through a
two-hour
SNOOZEFEST.

Hey, I might
as well have
comfy feet.

Brianna, Mom and I wore red dresses and matching

bows, while Dad wore a black suit with a red shirt and a big red-and-white polka-dotted bow tie.

I caught a glimpse of the four of us in the living room mirror and actually had a mini meltdown.

We looked like a family of, um . . . CIRCUS CLOWNS . . . all dressed up for a . . . clown . . . FUNERAL or something!

All we needed now was. . .

1. Some rubber balls for Dad

2. One of those trick plastic flowers that squirt water for Mom

3. A big plastic horn for Brianna AND

4. A little clown car for me, so I can jump in and drive away from my crazy family.

CLOWNS "R" US!

For some reason, Brianna's dress fit a little strangely.

Probably because it was on backwards. DUH!

"Brianna," Mom groaned. "I knew I shouldn't have let you put that on by yourself. Come here." She knelt down next to Brianna and adjusted her dress.

"No! I can dress myself!" Brianna protested. "I'm a big girl! My birthday is coming up soon, and I'm going to get a Princess Sugar Plum chocolate cake."

Mom just ignored her. "There," she said. "Now you look just as lovely as the Sugar Plum Fairy. She'll be in the ballet tonight."

"Hey!" Brianna's eyes lit up. "Is she Princess Sugar Plum's SISTER?"

Mom and Dad winked at each other.

"It's very possible," Mom said. "We're going to see her and her ballerina friends dance in pretty costumes. It's going to be a lot of fun. You'll see."

"Nikki, tell me the story about Princess Sugar Plum's sister? Please!" Brianna begged.

I rolled my eyes. It was a complicated story. And Brianna had the attention span of a Tater Tot.

?!

TATER TOT

← BRIANNA

"Well, her friend Clara gets a lame toy, her brother breaks it, it comes to life, their house gets infested with dancing rats and they visit a land full of sweets and desserts. Then their world gets taken over by an evil Rat King," I muttered.

"SWEETS and DESSERTS?!" Brianna squealed, basically ignoring everything I'd said about doom, gloom and dancing rodents. "Do you think there's chocolate cake there?"

"There's every dessert you can imagine," Mom added dreamily. "The flowers, trees and castles are all made of sweets. Doesn't that sound amazing?"

We all piled into the car, and about thirty minutes later we arrived at this huge, swanky-looking theatre. Everyone there had on suits and formal dresses.

Mom had managed to get us seats really close to the stage so we'd have a good view. But guess who got stuck sitting next to Brianna?

ME!!

I think Mom and Dad did that on purpose, because while the orchestra was warming up, they left their seats to go chat with friends.

I mean, WHO did they think I was? Mary Poppins?! Nanny McPhee?!

While Brianna and I were sitting there, she suddenly started swinging her feet and kicking the seat in front of us while singing a superobnoxious song she'd made up:

"Sugar plums, cookies and sweets
But watch out, Mr Rat
'Cause if you touch my chocolate cake
I'll whack you with a bat!"

An older man wearing a tux turned around and gave us BOTH a dirty look.

Which made no sense whatsoever because I wasn't the one singing and kicking his seat!

"Brianna," I hissed, "stop kicking that man's seat. And please be quiet!"

"Hi, Mr Bald Guy! How did you get your head to shine like that? Guess what? I'm wearing a new dress. On my birthday I'm going to get a chocolate—"

502

"Brianna! Zip it!" I snapped.

Finally Mom and Dad came back to their seats and the theatre lights dimmed.

But Brianna was already bored out of her skull.

When the orchestra started playing, she must have decided it was the perfect music for her little song because she started singing at the top of her lungs:

> "Sugar plums, cookies and sweets
> But watch out, Mr Rat—"

"Shhh!" At least a dozen frowning people shushed her.

I sank down in my seat and pretended I was with another family.

That's when Mom shot us BOTH a Death Stare.

Which made no sense whatsoever.

I wasn't the one singing about a RAT, really loudly and off-key.

All throughout the first act Brianna squirmed and kicked the seat in front of her.

But at least she was quiet.

Thank goodness.

Until the evil Rat King and his minions appeared.

That's when Brianna stood up in her chair, pointed at the stage, and screamed:

"Holy McNuggets! Those dancing rats are HUGE! And guess what?! My sister had a Halloween costume like that! Didn't you, Nikki? Except yours was really stinky. . . !"

Everyone turned and shot us dirty looks.

OMG! I was SO embarrassed.

I wanted to DIE!

I did NOT appreciate Brianna telling all of my personal business like that.

Hey, I didn't know those people.

They were, like, complete . . . STRANGERS!

Anyway, I think Brianna must have messed up the Rat King's concentration or something because he missed quite a few of his dance steps.

"So, where's Princess Sugar Plum's sister?" Brianna blurted out next.

"Brianna! Shhhh!" Mom scolded her in a whisper.

"Nikki, please try to keep your sister quiet, okay?" Dad pleaded under his breath.

"I am. She's just NOT listening!" I huffed kind of loudly.

Oops. I forgot to use my "inside" voice.

"SHHHHHHHH!!" At least a dozen people shushed me.

Finally the curtains came down and the lights went on for intermission.

OMG! It seemed like the entire audience was staring at us all evil-like.

"This is why you don't bring children to the theatre," the bald guy in the tux muttered loudly to his wife, followed by a few not-so-nice words.

Brianna tapped him on his shoulder again.

"Hey, Mr Baldy! Did you see those huge rats up on that stage?! Boy, were they scary!"

That was the last straw for the tux guy.

He turned really red, stood up, stomped over to an usher and demanded that he and his wife be given new seats.

I wanted to grab hold of his coat-tails, drop to my knees and beg desperately, "Please, sir, take me with you. Please!"

I had to get a break from Brianna before I totally lost it.

"I'll be right back!" I said to my parents. "I'm going to find some water. Or a ride home, if I'm lucky."

"Wait, Nikki! I wanna go toooo!" Brianna whined.

"I'll be right back, Brianna."

"But I need to go to the toilet!"

"Nikki, could you take your sister to the toilet? Please?" Mom asked.

DARN IT!!

I wanted to argue with Mom. But if Brianna had an accident while we were discussing the matter, I knew Mom was going to blame me.

And I was pretty sure the concessions stand DIDN'T sell Pampers in her size.

"Come on, Brianna!" I grumped.

"Thank you, dear!" Mom smiled. "I appreciate it."

Once we got to the toilets, I tried my best to be patient with Brianna.

"Now, hurry up and go, okay? The show will be starting again soon, and we want to get back to our seats before they dim the lights."

"Don't rush me!" Brianna said, and stuck her tongue out at me.

As she walked into the cubicle her eyes lit up. . .

"Oh, goody! Now I can pretend my arm is broken and wrap it up," she squealed happily.

Just great! I sighed.

This was going to take FOREVER!

I waited for three long minutes.

"Brianna, are you done yet?"

"Almost. Now I'm wrapping up my broken head."

"Your broken WHAT?! Brianna, let's GO! NOW!"

"But I STILL have to go to the toilet!"

"Fine! I'll be waiting for you on that bench right outside the door. When you get done, wash your hands and come right out. Okay?"

"Okay! Um, Nikki, do you have any . . . glue?"

I made a mental note-to-self: If, during my

lifetime, Mom EVER asks me to take Brianna to the toilet again, run away SCREAMING!

I hadn't been sitting on the bench for more than a minute when I noticed a long line of people waiting to buy these huge gourmet cupcakes in a fancy glass display case on the other side of the lobby.

I guess Brianna's obsessive rambling about chocolate cake must have affected my subconscious or something.

Because I could almost hear the double-fudge chocolate cupcakes calling my name.

Soon the line had dwindled down to two people, and Brianna was still nowhere in sight.

That's when I decided to make a mad dash to buy a cupcake.

It wasn't my fault that looking after Brianna meant I had worked up a tremendous appetite.

They were way overpriced at $7.00 each.

But they were the most-large, most-moist, most-luscious, most-chocolaty cupcakes I had ever seen in my entire life.

The sales clerk guy placed it in a fancy white box, and I carefully placed it in my purse.

Of course, me being the responsible older sister that I was, I never took my eyes off that toilet door for more than a few seconds (or minutes).

I started to get a little worried because they were flashing the house lights, which meant the interval was about to end.

And I was STILL waiting for Brianna to come out of the toilets.

So you can imagine my surprise when I turned around and spotted a frilly red Princess Sugar Plum dress at the drinking fountain on the other side of the lobby.

I rushed right over.

"There you are, Brianna! You were in the toilet FOREVER! We need to get back to our seats right now. Come on!"

I grabbed her hand and pulled her through the lobby.

That's when she stared up at me with the most HORRIFIED look on her face.

My brain was STILL trying to figure out how Brianna had gotten curly red hair, freckles and glasses.

But my mouth came up with the answer and suddenly blurted . . .

"Hey! You're NOT Brianna!"

"Mommy!" the little girl cried. "Stranger danger! Stranger danger!"

NOT ACTUALLY BRIANNA
↓

Startled, I dropped her hand and backed away.

"My bad!" I apologised. "I thought you were someone else! Sorry!"

Then I rushed back to the toilets to try to find my little sister.

"Brianna? Are you in here? Brianna!" I screamed as I checked every cubicle. But she was nowhere to be found.

My heart started to pound and my palms got really sweaty. I frantically ran back out into the hall and scanned the lobby. Still no Brianna.

That's when I started to panic. OMG! What if she's lost FOREVER?! The terrifying thought overwhelmed me.

I couldn't imagine life without my little sister, even though she was a Category 5 hurricane in pigtails.

I was so distraught, I even started to miss Miss Penelope.

I vowed that if I found Brianna, I'd buy a new purple pen and personally give Miss Penelope a glamorous makeover.

But now I had to go back into that theater and tell Mom and Dad I had somehow lost Brianna. I was ~~hoping~~ PRAYING Brianna had just wandered back into the auditorium.

If only she was back in her seat, safe and sound, torturing the people sitting nearby by kicking their seats, singing her obnoxious little song and chatting with Mr Baldy.

The ballet had already started up again by the time I got to my row. This meant I had to crawl over about a dozen highly annoyed people.

"Excuse me. I need to get through. Was that your foot? Sorry! I apologise. Oops!"

By the time I got to my seat, my eyes were finally starting to adjust to the darkness. I fully expected to see Brianna come into focus at any second.

"What took you so long?" Mom whispered really loudly. "We were starting to worry! Um, Nikki, dear . . . WHERE'S BRIANNA?!!"

I opened my mouth, but at first no words came out.

"She's not here? I thought maybe she came back to her seat!"

Mom's expression shifted from curiosity to alarm.

"WHAT?!" she said even louder.

Of course, everyone shot her dirty looks.

"I—I was waiting for her, and she just . . . VANISHED!"

"Did you check all the cubicles?"

"YES! Three times."

"Uh, dear. . ." Dad tapped Mom's arm nervously. His eyes were frozen on the stage.

"How about the lobby and the concessions stand?" Mom continued. "Maybe she saw some sweets."

"Mom, I looked EVERYWHERE!"

"Well, let's not panic. Maybe she's playing in the lifts. Let's go back out to the lobby and—"

"DEAR, you REALLY need to see this!" Dad interrupted again.

"What could possibly be more important right now than trying to find. . ."

That's when Mom and I looked up at the stage. "BRIANNA!!" we both screamed.

Clara and the Nutcracker prince were making
their grand entrance to the Land of Sweets in an
extravagant boat.

With a little stowaway in the backseat. Who was
festively draped in what looked like a full roll of
toilet paper.

"Brianna!" Mom called out to her.

But either Brianna couldn't hear Mom or she was ignoring her.

Brianna seemed almost hypnotised by the candy cane trees, gumdrop bushes and the humongous cupcake castle on the stage.

But the really scary part was that she had this mischievous grin that went from ear to ear.

The confused audience immediately noticed Brianna onstage in her toilet-paper outfit.

Most of them scratched their heads and whispered to each other.

No one seemed to remember there being a pint-sized mummy in *The Nutcracker*.

Clara and the Nutcracker prince, still all smiles, stared back at the audience with perplexed looks on their faces.

But when they finally turned and saw Brianna
standing there smiling and waving at the audience,
they totally FREAKED. . .

BRIANNA

Clara frantically whispered something to the prince.

He then leaned over, picked up Brianna and tried to carry her off the stage. But Brianna stubbornly held on to the boat for dear life. Finally he gave up and just left her there.

When the dancers took the stage, they didn't notice Brianna right away either.

Some of them were dressed as cookies and others as sweets. Then came the dancing chefs holding trays of pies, cupcakes and assorted pastries.

"That's what I'm talking 'bout!" Brianna screamed, and jumped out of the boat.

She bolted for the dancers like a crazy bull.

Mom, Dad and I ran towards the stage as fast as we could.

The moment felt surreal and like we were moving in slow motion.

"BRIANNA!" Mom cried. "NOOOOO!"

But there was no way we could get there before she started her feeding frenzy.

First, she grabbed a male dancer by the ankle and bit into his chocolate boot.

She made a face. "Yuck! That's NOT chocolate!"

The dancer shook her off his leg.

Next, Brianna ran to a candyfloss ballerina and grabbed her tutu.

The ballerina stopped dancing and tugged back.

But a piece of her tutu ripped off in Brianna's hand, and Brianna shoved it into her mouth. "Eww!" She spat it out and frowned. "That's NOT candyfloss!"

Almost all the characters stopped dancing and scrambled off the stage to avoid being eaten alive. Soon the only dancer left was a clueless chef

carrying a huge chocolate cake. He was totally
focussed on executing a series of grand pliés.

"Run! Run!" the frenzied audience chanted excitedly.

I couldn't believe it!

I expected people would be walking out, booing, or at least throwing rotten veggies.

But their butts were glued to their seats, and their eyes to the stage like they were watching the last ten minutes of a football game and the score was tied.

Brianna spotted the huge cake and just stared at it in awe.

When the chef finally caught a glimpse of Brianna, he suddenly stopped dancing and looked like he was about to wet his pants!

Brianna ran across the stage and lunged for the chef like a football player making a tackle.

The chef screamed, threw the chocolate cake up in the air and dove into the orchestra pit.

There was a crash and a loud, off-key note from the tuba.

It was quite obvious what musician the dancing chef had landed on.

Brianna triumphantly grabbed the cake and took a huge bite out of it just as we made it to the stage.

"Brianna, you come down here this instant!" Mom ordered.

Brianna lifted her head from the cake.

Her face was smeared with chocolate frosting, and her mouth was so full she looked like a blowfish.

After chewing for a few seconds, she frowned.

Perplexed and disappointed, Brianna pointed at the fake pastry. "Thith isn'th thocolate cake!" she said.

I barely made out what she was saying, but I saw white Styrofoam where she'd bitten a huge chunk out of the cake.

"There's no real food up here. It's all just props," I scolded. "I can't believe you did this!"

"Iz this a joke? Noth funny!" She pouted.

"Brianna Lynn Maxwell!" Mom shouted, and gave her the Death Stare. "Don't make me come up there. . .!"

Uh-oh! Mom meant business.

"Yeth, ma'am," Brianna finally mumbled in defeat.

She spat out the faux cake and jumped from the stage into Mom's arms.

Then the most shocking thing happened.

The dancers, the orchestra AND the audience gave Mom a standing ovation for single-handedly bringing the *Nutcracker* catastrophe to an end.

And get this!

After Brianna had pretty much obliterated the *Nutcracker* ballet, she actually had the nerve to wave and blow kisses to everyone, like she was on a TV show or something.

I felt a lot better when a ten-minute interval was announced so the dancers could prepare to start the second act over again.

And then the house lights came on.

As we left the theatre the audience was still laughing and cheering for Brianna, including Mr Baldy.

It was hard to believe those stuffy folks actually loved the *Nutcracker* ballet as a slapstick comedy.

We piled into the car and drove home in silence.

Mostly because no one had the energy to lecture Brianna.

If she had been MY child, I would have dropped her off at the nearest mental hospital for a psychiatric evaluation.

Or, better yet, the city zoo.

But she WASN'T my child. Thank goodness!

Even though I wanted to be angry at Brianna, deep down I was happy and relieved that she was okay.

It felt good to be home again. But my poor mom and dad were so exhausted they went straight to bed.

Being the responsible older daughter that I am, I assured my parents I would see to it that Brianna got into her pj's and safely tucked in.

I was surprised that she didn't whine and complain like she usually does at bedtime. She just hung her head, trudged upstairs and changed into her SpongeBob pyjamas.

I felt kind of sorry for her. In a way, all of this was mostly our fault. We had overemphasized the whole sugary-dessert theme of *The Nutcracker*.

Brianna was just a little kid. How was she supposed to know all the scenery and the chocolate cake was fake?

That's when I suddenly remembered MY cupcake, and my mouth started to water all over again.

I rushed downstairs to pour myself a tall, cold glass of milk.

I couldn't wait to get back to my room and sink my teeth into that luscious chocolaty cupcake while I wrote in my diary.

When I passed Brianna's room, I could tell she was still pretty upset. Even with her door closed, I could hear her sniffling and muttering to herself.

However, I froze in my tracks when I heard her sing what had to be the saddest song EVER:

"No sugar plums, cookies or sweets
The cupcake castle was flat
The chocolate cake was really fake
Sometimes I'm . . . such a . . . BRAT!"

I carefully placed my cupcake and glass of milk on the floor in front of her door. . .

Then I knocked on her door.

By the time Brianna opened it, I'd already dashed to my room and flopped across my bed.

I heard her squeal in delight!

"CHOCOLATE CAKE?! Thank you, Princess Sugar Plum! You made my WISH come true!"

"You're welcome!" I said aloud to myself, and smiled.

Who would have thunk this night would turn out so well?

Brianna DIDN'T end up on the side of a milk carton as a missing child.

The audience seemed to enjoy her antics in that wacky comedy-ballet-reality show.

And Mom and Dad were too exhausted to ground me for the rest of my life for losing Brianna.

But most importantly, I discovered that giving away something you cherish to someone you love can actually make you happier than keeping it.

I guess that's what Christmas is all about.

Oh, crud! I think I'm starting to sound like one of Mom's sappy greeting cards.

Hmmm, maybe my family isn't so BAD after all.

NOT!! ☺!!

ME, GIVING MY KOOKY FAMILY A BIG HUG!

When we got home from church this morning, it was snowing like crazy. And by noon there was at least ten centimetres.

As far as I was concerned, it was the perfect weather to curl up in front of the fireplace and sip hot chocolate with marshmallows.

But NOOO! My parents FORCED me to go outside in near-blizzard conditions for the STUPIDEST reason.

They wanted to build a snowman for Brianna!

Mom got all excited and said it would be a wonderful project for Family Sharing Time. But I already knew it was going to be a major DISASTER.

It was Dad's bright idea to make a life-size snowman. He was off to a really good start as his snowball grew bigger and bigger and bigger.

Then, unfortunately, he lost control of it on a hill. . .

?!

SO, ARE WE HAVING FUN YET?

EEK!!

DAD →

Well, there was good news and bad news.

The GOOD news was that Brianna ended up with a life-size snowman just like Dad had promised her.

But the BAD news was that DAD was the life-size snowman.

After he ran down that big hill, he dived headfirst into this huge snowbank. Then his snowball landed right on top of him. *CRUNCH!!*

OMG!! It took us ten minutes just to dig him out.

And by the time we got to him, he had NEW frostbite on top of the OLD frostbite he'd got from the snowblower fiasco.

I felt SO sorry for him. Especially since he was run over by that snowball while trying to do something nice for Brianna.

I just hope Dad isn't traumatized and suffering from some weird illness like snowman-a-phobia.

At this point, I don't think we're going to be building any more snowmen anytime soon.

Thank goodness!

Which allows me even MORE free time to curl up in front of the fireplace, drink hot chocolate with marshmallows and write in my DIARY.

I almost forgot! I STILL need to go shopping and buy a few more presents.

I've decided to give Brandon a Christmas present too. He's SUCH a sweetheart!

I just have to figure out something he'd really like.

Hmmm. Maybe a gift certificate for a romantic spaghetti dinner for TWO at Giovanni's!

SQUEEEE!!

☺!!

Every year, I wait until the very last minute to do my Christmas shopping. I sneak out of the house with Brianna, and we ride my bike in the snow to the nearest store. . .

Since I don't have my driver's licence yet, we're basically forced to shop at the closest place we can get to before we catch PNEUMONIA.

That's why Mom and Dad always get tacky presents, like a family-size pack of toothbrushes from me and gummy vitamins from Brianna.

"GIRLS!! YOU SHOULDN'T HAVE!!"

But this year I wanted to get them something special that they'd REALLY like.

You know, in addition to the toothbrushes and vitamins.

I was SO happy when I saw this huge bin of scrapbooks on sale!

It was BUY ONE, GET FOUR FREE! I was really lucky to stumble upon such a great holiday sale.

Or maybe the store was just trying to pawn them off on unsuspecting customers so there'd be less junk to throw away at the end of the shopping season.

Anyway, seeing those scrapbooks really got my creative juices flowing.

I decided to buy one as a gift for Mom and Dad. I planned to use my advanced skills in arts and crafts to create a beautiful new cover. It would be PERFECT for our family photos.

And since I was getting four extra scrapbooks for FREE, I decided to give one to Chloe, Zoey, Brianna and Brandon, too.

Was I not BRILLIANT ☺?!

I'd make Chloe and Zoey each a special scrapbook about our friendship.

And I knew Brianna would love anything with Princess Sugar Plum on the cover.

But then I started thinking about Brandon. What if he actually ended up moving away?

I wanted to give him something to remind him of our friendship and all the fun times we'd had.

Like the art competition, the Halloween party and the talent show. And even that time I actually thought I'd lost my diary at school!

Suddenly I started feeling really sad, right there in the Cold, Flu & Allergy medicine aisle.

I really wanted to help Brandon by skating in the *Holiday on Ice* show.

But I was also scared to death that I couldn't pull it off.

If only I could find someone to skate in my place!

I sighed and tried to swallow the huge lump in my throat.

Sometimes it felt like I was carrying the weight of the world on my shoulders.

Just as I was about to go through the checkout, I saw a familiar face in the lip gloss section of the cosmetics aisle.

It was MACKENZIE!!

My heart skipped a beat! Maybe there was hope for Brandon after all. If I put aside my ego and simply ~~asked~~ BEGGED her for help, maybe she would consider skating in my place.

"OMG! Hi, MacKenzie! I didn't know you shopped here," I said all friendlylike.

She looked at me and scowled. "Nikki, what are YOU doing here? Why aren't you hanging out with your dorky little friends at McTacoHut or somewhere?" she said.

I was dreading our conversation would go like this. But it was my fault. I should have appealed to her huge ego and opened with flattery.

"I absolutely love your lip gloss. The colour brings out the highlights in your eyes," I gushed.

"Well, you should try that new peachy colour. It'll complement your moustache hairs."

I could NOT believe she said that right to my face.

"Hey, I've seen PIGS wear lip gloss and look better than you!" I muttered under my breath.

"WHAT did you just say?!" she snapped.

547

We stared at each other. It was SO AWKWARD!

I needed her help so I lied through my teeth. "I said, 'Hey! I see PINK lip gloss looks good on YOU.'"

"Um, why are you even talking to me, Nikki?"

"Well, it's about *Holiday on Ice*. I know you wanted to skate for Fuzzy Friends. And now I'm having second thoughts."

"You're actually having thoughts? I'm impressed."

I just ignored her comment.

"MacKenzie, I want to ask you a big favour?"

"What? A donation to your plastic-surgery fund for the removal of moustache hair?"

I ignored THAT comment too.

"Would you take my place and skate with Zoey and Chloe for *Holiday on Ice*? We really need that money to keep Fuzzy Friends open."

"I'm surprised you didn't just ask me."

"I've wanted to ask you since last week. You're one of the best skaters in the show. If I mess this up, Brandon will be crushed. And it'll all be my fault."

MacKenzie looked amused and smiled. "YES! You're absolutely correct!" she said.

"OMG! Is that a YES, you'll skate for me?" I exclaimed happily.

I could NOT believe MacKenzie had actually said yes! It was a MIRACLE!

"NO! That's a YES, that Brandon will be CRUSHED and it will be YOUR fault! Sorry, Nikki! But if you were on FIRE, I wouldn't SPIT on you!"

"What about Brandon? Then at least do it for him. If anything happens to Fuzzy Friends, he's going to be heartbroken!"

"I know!" she said smugly. "Actually, I'm counting on

it! WHO is going to be there for Brandon when he needs a shoulder to cry on after his STUPID little shelter closes? ME! That's who! And the best part is that he's going to HATE YOU for letting him down. And that's just the way I want it!"

Then MacKenzie cackled like a witch.

I just stood there in SHOCK!!

I could not believe anything breathing could be that EVIL.

It's quite obvious that MacKenzie has set me up! AGAIN!! I'm SO sick of her little mind games!

But I'm NOT going to get MAD!

I'm going to get EVEN!

By believing in myself and skating my BUTT off!

And I'm going to be STRONG! And FIERCE! And, of course, wear a SUPERCUTE outfit!

I'll be more deadly than that Terminator guy.

I'm going to be. . .

THE SKATER-NATOR

ME↘

Anyway, all the scrapbooks I made turned out really cute.

And the pages Brianna decorated for Mom and Dad were, um . . . quite . . . interesting.

Me, Nikki ♥

Brianna and Dad at Camp Caring.

Brianna as the Easter Bunny.

Love

I plan to wrap all the scrapbooks and then deliver Chloe's and Zoey's on Christmas Eve.

I decided to just leave Brandon's in the mailbox at Fuzzy Friends since he spends so much time there anyway.

I think he's going to be supersurprised I actually made a special gift for him.

Now he'll have a special place to keep all his photos.

I just hope he likes it.

☺!

TUESDAY, DECEMBER 24

Today is Christmas Eve!

One of Mom's favourite winter craft projects is knitting matching sweaters for our family.

This year it's a fairly hideous snowman sweater with a string of plastic ornaments trimming the collar.

The sweater is blue and has one red sleeve, one green sleeve and a huge 3-D snowman on the front.

Our names were knitted in fifteen-centimetres-tall yellow letters across the back.

I thought about sending mine off to *Guinness World Records* as an entry for Ugliest Sweater in the History of Mankind.

I didn't care about setting a record. I just wanted to get rid of the darn thing before someone actually made me wear it. But it was too late. . .

HEY, HONEY! LET'S TAKE A FAMILY PICTURE
IN THESE PRETTY SWEATERS!

Dad set up his camera, and we gathered in front of our Christmas tree.

Then he set the timer and quickly took his place next to Mom.

"Okay! Everyone say 'Cheese!'" he said.

However, right before the flash went off, Brianna must have decided she wanted a little snack or something.

Because suddenly she turned and yanked at a candy cane hooked on a tree branch.

OMG! I couldn't believe the whole tree fell over.

It was totally a Maxwell family moment.

I laughed so hard my ribs hurt.

I have to admit, this family portrait is now my favourite.

Unfortunately, Mom decided we looked SO
ADORABLE in our snowman sweaters, she wants
us all to wear them to dinner at my aunt Mabel's
house tomorrow.

I was like, JUST GREAT ☹!! My aunt Mabel is NOT exactly my favourite relative.

It was going to be like having dinner with AUNTY SCROOGE!

THIS is the woman who STILL insists that I sit at the dreaded KIDDIE TABLE!

Any holiday spirit I had, leaked right out of me.

Just thinking about the kiddie table made me so anxious I thought I was going to have a complete meltdown.

To survive this ordeal, I was going to need nothing short of a Christmas miracle!

Today is Christmas Day!

Brianna woke us up by banging on our bedroom doors and screaming hysterically.

Just like she does every year.

And it's always the EXACT same story. . .

"Wake up, everybody! Wake up! Me and Miss Penelope just saw Santa and his reindeer leaving. They flew right off our roof and over Mrs Wallabanger's house. Wake up! It's an emergency!"

Then we all rush downstairs in our pyjamas to see

what Santa has left and open our presents together.

As usual, Brianna got a ton of stuff. . .

Mom and Dad LOVED the scrapbook that Brianna
and I made (which included that hilarious photo of
our Christmas tree falling over). . .

MOM & DAD, LOVING THEIR SCRAPBOOK

But the very BEST present was . . .

MY BRAND-NEW PHONE!!

Soon it was time to go to my aunt Mabel's for our holiday dinner. Dad says his oldest sister is just old-fashioned and kind of strict. But I think "strict" is just a nicer word for "MEAN".

Mom says Aunt Mabel acts like that because she thinks kids should be seen and not heard.

Personally, I think Aunt Mabel just HATES kids because she has nine of them.

OMG!! If I gave birth NINE whole times, I wouldn't want to SEE them or HEAR them! I'm just sayin'.

But get this! I'm fourteen years old. And that EVIL woman STILL made me sit at the KIDDIE TABLE!

The adults sat in the dining room at a hand-carved antique table with Queen Anne chairs, fancy porcelain china, crystal glasses and gold-plated cutlery.

The kiddie table was a wobbly, child-size card table covered with a worn-out bedsheet.

We got paper plates, plastic forks and those teeny-tiny paper cups (you know, the ones you use in your bathroom when you brush your teeth).

And sitting at the kiddie table while wearing my snowman sweater meant I was twice as humiliated.

The whole thing was a very traumatic experience.

Thank goodness the food was delicious, or it would have been a totally worthless visit.

My aunt Mabel is as mean as a pit bull, but she's an excellent cook.

Anyway, I was really happy when we finally made it back home, because I got to play around with my new phone.

I CANNOT believe all the cool stuff it has, like Internet, texting, email, instant messaging, games, a camera, homework help, automatic pizza delivery and a teen-peer counselling hotline.

OMG! If my phone paid an ALLOWANCE, parents would be OBSOLETE!

Brianna went NUTS because my phone came with the game Princess Sugar Plum Saves Baby Unicorn Island. I let her play it for an hour right before bedtime and now she's, like, totally addicted.

My new phone is going to save me a ton of money.

Now whenever I need to bribe Brianna to do

something, I simply pay her with Princess Sugar Plum game minutes instead of cash.

It took me a while to figure it out, but I took a picture of me with my phone and sent it to Chloe, Zoey and Brandon.

They are going to be supershocked and surprised when they receive it.

Overall, my Christmas was pretty good.

It started snowing outside and actually looked like a winter wonderland.

Then Dad lit the fireplace and we all roasted

marshmallows together. Again! Only this time Dad's trousers didn't catch on fire.

I have to admit . . . Once you get used to them, having a family to hang out with can be kind of nice.

I wonder how Brandon's Christmas is going?

It's really admirable that he helps out his grandparents by volunteering at Fuzzy Friends. I throw a hissy fit when I have to clean my room and put dishes in the dishwasher.

I'm SUCH a spoiled BRAT! And I don't really appreciate the blessings I have, like my family.

It's just mind-boggling how he's lost pretty much everything, yet he continues to have so much to GIVE!

Now, THAT'S truly a CHRISTMAS MIRACLE!

☺!!

Today was our first practice session with Victoria Steel, the *Holiday on Ice* show director and Olympic gold medalist figure skater.

Everyone participating in the show received a welcome letter and a list of rules:

VICTORIA STEEL'S SHOW RULES

1. NO AUTOGRAPHS
2. NO GUM CHEWING
3. NO UGLY SKATING OUTFITS
4. NO HAIRY LEGS

All skaters are to be prompt, courteous and prepared.

Unsportsmanlike behavior will not be tolerated, and any violation will result in automatic dismissal from the *Holiday on Ice* show.

GOOD LUCK!
VICTORIA STEEL

All we have to do now is survive three days of practice with Victoria.

My biggest fear is that she's going to kick me out of the show like she did to that poor girl last year. Chloe insisted it was probably just a rumour, but I wasn't taking any chances. After scrounging around in our garage, I found the perfect costume for our first practice.

I was a nervous wreck when Mom dropped me off for practice at the ice arena.

All I could think of was Brandon having to start a new school in January without any friends.

Since I didn't want anyone to see my costume, I avoided the crowded locker room and got dressed in a small bathroom on the far side of the arena instead.

I stared at my reflection in the mirror and smiled. I knew I looked ridiculous.

But if my plan worked, at least I'd make it through the first practice.

By the time I made my way back to the rink, most of the skaters were already on the ice practising, including Chloe and Zoey.

I was amazed at how graceful they were, and I couldn't help but feel proud of them.

Near the main entrance, a large crowd surrounded Victoria. She was pretty and looked surprisingly similar to the girl on the cover of *The Ice Princess*.

Fans took pictures of her with their phones and waited in line for an autograph.

And like a pop star, she travelled with her own entourage and security detail.

As Victoria rushed past me she took off her sunglasses and let out an irritated sigh.

"Let's get this over with! I just hope this group

is better than last year's! Can someone get me a water? I'm about to die of thirst!"

Her staffers scrambled in different directions, and within thirty seconds two assistants and two security guys offered her bottled waters.

"OMG! You expect me to drink water from a PLASTIC bottle?" she shrieked.

One thing was quite obvious. The woman was a spoiled diva!

The assistant director asked all the skaters to take a seat in the first two rows.

He then introduced Victoria as the skaters cheered excitedly.

In spite of her meltdown over the bottled water situation, she immediately plastered a fake smile on her face.

"So! Who'd like to impress me first?" she asked,

eyeing the list of names on her clipboard. "Let's start with a group. How about. . ."

My heart skipped a beat.

Please don't call us! Please don't call us! Please don't call us! I chanted inside my head.

". . .Chloe, Zoey and Nikki. Front and centre!"

Chloe and Zoey quickly scrambled on to the ice.

"Why do I only see two of you, instead of three?" Victoria asked with a highly annoyed glare.

"Um . . . Nikki should be here. Somewhere!" Zoey answered, and glanced nervously at Chloe.

"Here I am," I said as I carefully made my way on to the ice.

Chloe and Zoey took one look at me, gasped and shrieked. . .

NIKKI, WHAT HAPPENED?!!

That's when I realised my fake cast made from toilet paper and tape actually looked pretty real. Especially with Dad's old crutches from that time he went bungee jumping.

"Don't worry. It's not as bad as it looks," I answered.

"OMG! Is it broken?" Chloe asked.

"You poor thing!" Zoey exclaimed.

"I'm FINE! REALLY!" I said, and kind of winked. Chloe and Zoey looked at me and then at each other. I think they got the hint.

"So, you're Nikki?" Victoria asked, staring me down. "I'm really sorry about your accident, but I have a show to run here. You three are just going to have to participate next year. Sorry, girls!"

"NO! PLEASE! Actually, it's just a little sprain. My doctor assured me I'd be fine by—by, um . . . tomorrow," I stammered.

That's when Victoria suddenly narrowed her eyes at my cast and stared at me suspiciously. "So, your doctor uses TAPE?!" Then she put her hands on her hips and yelled . . .

I could NOT believe that crazy lady actually called security on me like that. She's NUTZ!!

"Chloe and Zoey, get into position — now! I want to see this routine!" she shouted. "But I'm warning you! If the THREE of you are NOT ready to skate tomorrow, you'll be disqualified! Understood?"

We nodded.

As I hurried off the ice, I gave Chloe and Zoey a thumbs-up, and they smiled at me nervously. As long as I wasn't out there messing things up, they were going to do fine.

And I was right. They both skated flawlessly, and Victoria was both surprised and impressed.

I decided not to hang around for the rest of the practice session. I'd had quite enough of Victoria Steel for one day and I was sure the feeling was mutual.

I hobbled back to the bathroom, anxious to ditch the uncomfortable crutches and itchy cast. I was about to call my mom to pick me up, when an uninvited guest barged in.

It was MACKENZIE!! And boy, was she ticked!

I was going to bat my eyes all innocentlike and completely DENY the whole fake-cast thing.

But then I realised my crutches were leaning against the wall and I was standing there perfectly fine on my "injured" ankle.

OOPS!!

Phoney or not, MY personal health issues were none of MacKenzie's business.

"You're calling ME a phoney?" I huffed. "You're wearing SO many hair extensions and SO much lip gloss, the fire warden has declared you a fire hazard due to a high risk of spontaneous combustion!"

OMG! MacKenzie was so angry I thought her head was going to explode.

She stared at me with her beady little eyes and hissed, "I've already warned Victoria about you. Make one more wrong step and she'll throw you out of this show faster than a ten-day-old mouldy pizza."

Then she turned and sashayed away.

I hate it when MacKenzie sashays!

I could NOT believe she was trying to boss me around like that. I mean, just WHO does she think she is?! The ICE-SKATING POLICE?!

Anyway, the good news is that I actually survived the first *Holiday on Ice* practice session with Victoria the Dragon Lady.

ONE down and TWO more to go.

☺!!

After Victoria threatened us yesterday, I didn't dare show up with that fake cast again.

I had tossed and turned most of the night, trying to come up with another plan.

But the sad truth was that it was pretty much over for me.

As soon as Victoria took one look at me ~~skating~~ scooting around on the ice, she was going to kick Chloe, Zoey and me right out of her show.

And it didn't help that MacKenzie was probably telling her awful stuff about me. Like I stole Fuzzy Friends from her and my broken leg was fake.

Well, okay! So maybe the broken leg thing WAS fake. But still! It was none of that girl's business.

When Victoria started screaming at the music guy, the lights guy and the wardrobe guy (OMG! That crazy lady did A LOT of SCREAMING), I decided to sneak away and hide out up in the stands for a few minutes.

Then I could have my massive panic attack in private.

I was deep in thought, pondering my hopeless situation, when a very familiar voice startled me.

"So, what does it feel like to be an Ice Princess?"

"BRANDON! What are you doing here?" I gasped.

"I came to thank you for making me that awesome scrapbook! And to cheer on Team Fuzzy Friends!"

This guy was too nice to be real! The possibility that he might move away was just . . . too depressing!

Suddenly I was overcome with emotion. I had to bite my lip to keep from bursting into tears.

Brandon's warm smile slowly vanished, and he just stared at me in silence.

"Nikki! Are you okay? What's wrong. . . ?"

"I'm sorry, Brandon! But I don't know if I'm going to be able to earn that money to help Fuzzy Friends. I'm just . . . SO sorry! I really am!"

"What do you mean? No one expects you to be a pro. Just being in the show is enough."

"NO! It's NOT. I have to be able to SKATE in the show. And I CAN'T! But I didn't know that at the time I volunteered to help. Honest!"

"Come on, Nikki! You CAN'T be that bad!"

"Brandon, listen to me. I'm THAT bad! No! Actually, I'm WORSE! I seriously expect to get kicked out of the show after we skate today."

Brandon blinked his eyes in disbelief.

"Victoria requires that skaters be prepared to skate and I'm NOT! I can barely stand on the ice, let alone skate on it!"

We just sat there in silence as the sheer hopelessness of my situation sank in.

If I DIDN'T skate, Fuzzy Friends would close and Brandon would be moving!

And if I DID skate, Fuzzy Friends would close and Brandon would be moving!

It was a LOSE—LOSE situation.

"I'm sorry, Nikki. I wish there was something I could do. . ." Brandon muttered as he stared down at Victoria, who was now screaming at the guy resurfacing the ice.

My heart started to pound when she announced over the speaker system that Chloe, Zoey and I were up next.

Brandon gave me a weak smile.

"Break a leg! Actually, try NOT to break a leg! Sorry."

"Thanks!" I said, smiling at his little joke.

Brandon didn't know that I'd ALREADY tried using that "broken leg" thing on Victoria.

Been there, done that!

When I got down to the rink, I could tell Chloe and Zoey were supernervous too, but they were trying their best not to show it.

"Okay, Team Fuzzy! Group hug!" Chloe said, and did her jazz hands to try to lighten the mood.

Somehow I made it on to the ice and got into position without falling.

And just as our music began, I saw Brandon approach Victoria with his camera and tap her on her shoulder.

When she turned around, he introduced himself and pointed to his camera.

Apparently, Victoria was immediately charmed by his professionalism, good manners and smile.

Which was a really good thing, because our skating routine was NOT going so well. . .

BRANDON, PHOTOGRAPHING VICTORIA WHILE I FALL ON MY FACE

Coincidentally (or not), Brandon's impromptu photo shoot lasted until the final note of our music.

And when Victoria FINALLY turned around . . .

We plastered big smiles on our faces and struck a superFIERCE pose. Like we were the top three finalists on *America's Next Top Model* or something.

No one ever would have guessed I had just fallen four times during our three-minute routine.

OMG! I'd spent so much time sliding around on my BUTT, it had frostbite.

Victoria just stared at us with this strange look on her face as we held our breath.

"Great job, girls!!" she finally said, and turned to her assistant. "WHERE is my cappuccino? Am I supposed to run this show AND do YOUR job?!"

Brandon gave me a huge smile and winked.

I wanted to MELT into a puddle right there on the ice.

Of course, when I walked past MacKenzie, she glared at me and held her nose.

But I already knew I completely STANK as a skater.

She didn't have to remind me.

Anyway, I CANNOT believe we're STILL in the show.

Brandon is such a SWEETHEART!! I could not believe he helped us out like that.

TWO practice sessions DOWN.

And ONE to go!

WOO-HOO!!

☺!!

SATURDAY, DECEMBER 28

BRIANNA AND I GO SLEDDING
(A TERRIFYING EXPERIENCE)

BRIANNA, ARE YOU SURE ABOUT
DEAD MAN'S DROP? IT MIGHT BE KINDA
SCARY FOR A LITTLE KID LIKE YOU!

THERE IT IS!

TO BE CONTINUED. . . !!
☹!!

SUNDAY, DECEMBER 29

BRIANNA AND I GO SLEDDING
(A TERRIFYING EXPERIENCE)
CONTINUED. . .

When we last saw our heroes, Brianna and Nikki, they were speeding down a towering cliff, about to plummet to their deaths. But just when it seemed like they were DOOMED. . .

My parents' priorities are totally screwed up.

Mom had to rush off to visit a friend who'd just had a baby.

And Dad had an emergency call from some rich lady whose fancy dinner party had been crashed by some unexpected guests. About two thousand ants!

Guess WHO got stuck babysitting Brianna?

ME! That's who!

Even though that meant I had to bring her with me to an EXTREMELY important practice session at the ice-skating arena that involved $3,000 and possibly LIFE and DEATH!

A new BABY is born somewhere in the world every seven seconds and ANTS will still be around even after a nuclear war.

HOW in the world was what THEY were doing MORE important than what I was doing?!

"Nikki, just call me when you're done with practice," Mom said as she pulled up in front of the arena. "And, Brianna, you be a good girl and listen to your sister, okay?"

"Okay, Mommy!" Brianna beamed like a little angel.

Then she turned and stuck her tongue out at me.

"Nikki, can I play Princess Sugar Plum on your phone?" Brianna asked as we entered the building.

It was the fifth time she had asked me that today.

"No, Brianna, you're here to watch the ice skaters."

Chloe and Zoey were already on the ice practising. But when they saw Brianna, they rushed over and gave her a big hug.

Brianna was fascinated by the skaters and sat

quietly and watched. I could hardly believe she was behaving so well.

About twenty-five minutes later Victoria called our names.

"We're up!" Zoey said with a nervous smile. "Are you ready, Nikki?"

I took a deep breath and stepped forwards to meet my destiny. I was so nervous, I thought I was going to lose my Egg McMuffin.

I'd managed to get through the first two practices without Victoria tossing me out.

But short of a major miracle, I thought it was finally the end of the line for me.

Once she actually saw me skate, or more correctly, TRY to skate, I was SO out of the show.

"Final call!" Victoria said sharply. "Chloe, Zoey and Nikki!"

As we hustled onto the ice, Victoria watched us like a hawk. I tried my hardest NOT to fall.

We were just about to get into our starting positions when suddenly there was a major disruption from the stands. . .

HEY, YOU GUYS, I WANNA SLIDE ON THE ICE TOO!

I skated over, grabbed Brianna's hand, and escorted her back to her seat!

"Brianna! Are you trying to get us kicked out of the show?" I hissed. "Sit right there and DON'T! MOVE!"

She gave me her saddest puppy-dog eyes. "But, Nikki! I want to slide on the ice with you, Chloe, and Zoey!"

Victoria looked like she was going to blow a gasket. But since there was a camera crew nearby, she just stretched her lips into a cold, mannequin-like smile and batted her eyes really fast.

As I turned to go back on the ice, a guy in a blue uniform stopped me.

"Excuse me, but I have a flower delivery for a Victoria Steel. It's from the mayor's office. I was told to leave them at the front desk, but it's closed. Do you know who she is?"

"Sure, she's right over there," I said, pointing.

Victoria appeared to be doing an impromptu live interview with a TV reporter.

"Well, I don't want to interrupt her. But I'm running behind schedule on my deliveries. Could you do me a favour and see to it that she gets these?"

"No problem!" I said.

He placed a beautiful bouquet of two dozen pink roses on the seat next to Brianna.

"Oooh! Those are really PRETTY!" Brianna squealed. "Are they yours?"

"No, they're for that lady over there!" I said, pointing to Victoria. "I have to give them to her."

"Nikki, can I give them to her?" Brianna asked excitedly.

"Don't even think about it! Stay in your seat!"

That's when I got the most brilliant idea!

"Actually, Brianna, it would be a BIG help if you'd take these flowers over to Victoria!" I said happily.

"Goody gumdrops!" she cheered.

"But I need you to be really careful with them. I'm going to wave at you when it's time. Okay?"

"Okay. Can I smell them too? I bet they smell like candyfloss! Or bubble gum!"

I took my place on the ice next to Chloe and Zoey, but I was so nervous, I couldn't think straight.

Just as the music was about to start, I waved at Brianna to signal her to take the flowers to Victoria.

Only Brianna just smiled and waved back at me.

I waved at her again and this time pointed at the flowers. But Brianna just waved and pointed at the flowers too.

JUST GREAT ☹!!

As music blared over the speakers, Chloe and Zoey moved gracefully over the ice.

But I stood there in my pose, waving my arms in slow motion and wishing I could skate over and strangle Brianna.

After what seemed like FOREVER, Brianna finally got a clue. She snatched up the bouquet of roses and trudged off toward Victoria.

Brianna tugged on Victoria's coat, and when the woman turned around, a wide smile spread across her face.

"Psst!" Chloe whispered. "Nikki! SKATE!"

I took off gliding across the ice, immediately lost my balance, and fell to my knees.

Brianna smiled and handed Victoria the bouquet of flowers.

"For me?" She gushed like she had just been awarded another gold medal or something.

Then I tripped over Chloe's foot, collided with Zoey and slid across the ice on my butt. It was . . . SURREAL!

Totally flattered by Brianna's borrowed gift, Victoria grabbed a pen and paper and gave Brianna her autograph.

And because Brianna was equally as vain as the celebrity skater, she insisted on giving Victoria HER autograph too.

Then Brianna gave Victoria a big hug.

Of course the TV cameras captured every second.

It seemed like all that gushing, hugging and smiling went on, like, FOREVER. Or at least, long enough for us to finish our routine.

Once again we struck a FIERCE ending pose and waited breathlessly for the verdict.

When Victoria finally turned around and faced us, she was practically glowing.

Hugging her bouquet in one arm and Brianna in the other, she smiled and said . . .

THAT WAS WONDERFUL!

YAY!

As Chloe, Zoey and I blinked in astonishment,
Brianna cheered for us. Very loudly.

But, hey! Who were WE to disagree with the great and wonderful Victoria Steel?

And her, um . . . trusty sidekick, Brianna!

So right now I'm NOT that mad at Mom and Dad about this whole babysitting thing.

The amazing thing is that I actually SURVIVED THREE whole practice sessions with THE Victoria Steel, BANSHEE DIVA of the figure skating world!

Now if I could just make it through our entire performance tomorrow, Fuzzy Friends Animal Rescue Centre will be saved and Brandon won't have to move away.

I'm so NOT looking forward to publicly humiliating myself by tripping, slipping and stumbling my way through our routine tomorrow.

But I'm willing to do whatever I have to do.

And I'm STILL really worried that MacKenzie is

going to pull some kind of stunt at the last minute to get us kicked out of the show.

Even though she hasn't said anything to me since our little blow-up a few days ago, every time I see her, she just stares at me the way a very hungry snake looks at a mouse.

That girl is RUTHLESS.

She'll do just about anything to anybody to get whatever she wants.

I will be SO relieved when the *Holiday on Ice* show is finally OVER!

☹!!

TUESDAY, DECEMBER 31

OMG! OMG! OMG! I cannot believe what just happened! I guess I should just start at the beginning. . .

The *Holiday on Ice* show is well-known for its fabulous costumes. And this year Victoria Steel borrowed them from the private collection of a famous, award-winning Broadway producer.

At 9:00 a.m., everyone met with the wardrobe manager for a final fitting and costume check.

Chloe, Zoey and I were skating to the classical holiday piece "Dance of the Sugar Plum Fairy" from *The Nutcracker*.

That was because Chloe and Zoey were dying to wear a superglitzy costume like the heroine in *The Ice Princess*.

Well, my BFFs got their wish! The fairy costumes Victoria selected for us were AMAZING!

I almost fell over in shock when MacKenzie actually complimented us.

She said she loved our gorgeous costumes and they were her very favourites.

After our fitting was over, we spent the morning at a swanky spa getting manicures and pedicures. Then we visited a salon for hair and makeup.

Talk about GLAM! We were ready for the cover of *Girls' Life* magazine!

After we grabbed a quick lunch, it was almost 2:00 p.m. and time to head back to the arena to get dressed for the 4:00 p.m. show.

Even though I was a nervous wreck about skating in front of a thousand people, my only goal was to finish that routine. Even if it killed me.

Then Fuzzy Friends would be awarded the money and Brandon could stay at WCD ☺!

But unfortunately, what started off as a great day was quickly ruined when we realised . . .

OUR SUGAR PLUM FAIRY COSTUMES WERE
MISSING!! AND IN THEIR PLACE WERE . . .

CLOWN COSTUMES?!

When we reported the situation to the wardrobe manager, she and her staff spent thirty minutes searching for our fairy costumes.

But they were nowhere to be found.

I had a sneaking suspicion MacKenzie had something to do with the disappearance.

She had this nasty little smirk on her face and was snickering at our new costumes. But I had no proof whatsoever.

Apparently, Victoria had ordered the clowns and three other costumes but had decided not to use them.

All the extra costumes had been picked up by a delivery service at noon to be transported back to New York City. But SOMEHOW our costumes and the clown ones had been switched.

This meant our beautiful Sugar Plum Fairy costumes were already halfway back to New York City by now.

We were devastated! Chloe and Zoey were so upset
they started to cry.

"Come on, guys!" I said. "Don't be upset. We can
STILL do this!"

"But I was really looking forward to being an Ice
Princess!" Chloe whimpered.

"Me too!" Zoey sniffed.

"But don't you see? This is about more than just
looking glamorous. We're doing this for Fuzzy Friends.

Remember?!" I said, trying to give them a pep talk.

"And, yes, I know!" I continued. "These clown costumes are freakishly ugly, and we'll probably look scary and a little insane. And the kids at school will make fun of us for the rest of the year, and we'll probably be an embarrassment to our parents. But look at the bright side. . ."

Chloe and Zoey looked at me expectantly. "What's the bright side?" they both asked.

"Well, um . . . actually. It's . . . um. Okay! So maybe there ISN'T a BRIGHT side! But a lot of nice people and cute little fuzzy animals are depending on us! Just ask yourself, what would Crystal Coldstone, the Ice Princess, do?"

Suddenly Chloe wiped her tears and placed her hands on her hips. "Well, Crystal would kick butt and send those Vambies packing! That's what she'd do!"

"And she'd wear a freakishly ugly clown costume if it meant saving humankind!" Zoey added.

Then Zoey lowered her voice to almost a whisper. "The art of the clown is more profound than we think . . . It is the COMIC mirror of tragedy, and the TRAGIC mirror of comedy — André Suarès."

FINALLY! I seemed to be getting through to my BFFs.

"Come on, girlfriends!" I said. "LET'S DO THIS THING!!"

That's when we did a group hug!

It was a little weird going from glamorous Sugar Plum Fairies to a pathetic clown posse, but as we got dressed we tried to keep a positive attitude.

In spite of the new costumes, we decided to keep our original music and skating routine.

Especially since we'd been practising it for the past two weeks.

Soon Mom and Brianna came back to the dressing room to wish us luck. When Brianna saw our new clown costumes, she got really excited.

"Hey, guess what? When I grow up, I'm going to slide on the ice and be a scary, stupid-looking clown too, just like you guys!" she gushed.

I think that was a compliment, but I'm not sure.

Brianna picked up my phone from the dressing room table, and her eyes lit up.

NIKKI, CAN I PLAY THE PRINCESS SUGAR PLUM GAME ON YOUR PHONE WHILE YOU, CHLOE AND ZOEY ARE SLIDING ON THE ICE?

"No, Brianna. I told you NEVER to touch my phone unless I say you can. Remember?"

"Pretty please!" Brianna whined. "I promise I won't break it." Then she shoved my phone behind her back so I couldn't reach it.

"MOM!" I whined even louder than Brianna.

"Brianna Maxwell!" Mom scolded. "You know the rule. Your sister's phone is off-limits unless she gives you permission. Now hand it over!"

Brianna gave Mom her saddest puppy-dog eyes and then pouted like a two-year-old. But she finally surrendered my phone, and I snatched it from her.

"Me and Miss Penelope think you're a MEANIE!" Brianna said, sticking her tongue out at me.

"Fine. Then YOU and MISS PENELOPE can NEVER, EVER play the Princess Sugar Plum game on MY phone for the rest of your LIVES! So THERE!"

Then I stuck my tongue out at both of them.

"Okay, girls! That's enough!" Mom scolded Brianna and me.

I placed my phone back on my dressing table.

But when I saw Brianna watching me like a hawk, I stuck it inside that cute little pocket on my bag and stuffed my bag in my backpack with the rest of my clothes.

Just as Mom and Brianna were leaving, the assistant stage manager announced that the show would be starting in forty-five minutes. All of us skaters had to check in with the stage manager across the hall.

"I gotta go to the toilet!" Brianna whined really loudly. "NOW!"

She was SUCH an embarrassment!

Chloe showed Brianna and Mom the door to the toilet in our dressing room.

Then we rushed off to check in.

When we came back to our dressing room to grab our skates and start warm-ups, we saw a note posted on the door.

> Chloe, Zoey and Nikki,
>
> Great news! We
> located your Sugar Plum
> Fairy costumes in Storage
> Area C in Locker 17.
>
> Please pick them up
> and get dressed ASAP!
>
> -V-

The wardrobe manager had found our costumes!
We were so happy, we did a group hug and started
screaming.

"OMG! They finally found them!" I screamed.

"Just in time!" Zoey screamed.

"We're going to be Ice Princesses after all!" Chloe screamed.

"LET'S GO!" I yelled as we took off running down the hall. "We only have thirty minutes before the show starts!"

Suddenly Chloe stopped.

"Wait! I'm going to grab my phone so we can call our moms and let them know they found our Sugar Plum Fairy costumes. Plus, we need to wash off the clown makeup and put on the fairy makeup, and we're going to need their help!"

"Great idea!" Zoey and I exclaimed.

Storage Area C was on the other side of the arena, near the hockey player locker rooms. All team practices had been cancelled due to the ice show, so the halls were dark, shadowy and strangely quiet.

"Is it me, or is this place kind of creepy?" Zoey said nervously.

"We're just going to grab our costumes and get out of here," Chloe assured her.

"Okay. Storage locker fourteen, fifteen, sixteen," I counted out loud, "and seventeen! Here it is, guys!"

The closet was closed by a simple latch on the outside.

We opened it and peered in. It was even darker inside.

"Don't be skurd!" I teased. "It's just a walk-in storage closet," I said as we all stepped inside.

"Is there a light in here?" Zoey asked.

"Hey! Let's use my phone," Chloe suggested. "It lights up!"

She held it up high in the centre of the storage area, and it cast an eerie green glow.

"Thanks, that's a lot better," I said. "Okay, I see hockey sticks, pucks and ice skates. But no Sugar Plum Fairy costu—"

The huge metal door suddenly slammed shut. Then I heard the outside latch slide into place.

KLA-CHUNK!

The clatter of quick footsteps echoed right outside the door and then down the long, empty hallway.

Chloe, Zoey and I stared at one another in horror as the gravity of our situation slowly sank in. Then we had a massive meltdown and started pounding on the metal door like crazy.

"Help! Someone! We're locked in here! Let us out! Help! Help!" we screamed frantically.

But it became quite clear pretty fast that whoever had locked us inside was not coming back anytime soon.

We'd been set up. There were never any Sugar Plum Fairy costumes in locker 17.

And all we could do was watch nervously as the green glow from Chloe's phone got dimmer and dimmer.

"Sorry, guys. I think I forgot to charge my phone.

But I think I can make three or four calls before it goes completely dead. Any suggestions?"

For about thirty seconds it was so quiet in the room you could hear a pin drop.

"Let's try calling our moms first," Zoey offered.

"Good idea!" Chloe and I agreed.

But it wasn't. All three of their phones went straight to voicemail. Which meant they were probably already turned off so as not to ring during the show.

Still, we each left a detailed message.

The GOOD news was that at the very worst, our moms would retrieve our messages AFTER the ice show was over and come looking for us.

So it was just a matter of time before we got rescued.

But the BAD news was that we were going to be

stuck in the storage locker for two very long, dark, spooky hours until they showed up.

"One call left. If we're lucky!" Chloe announced, staring at her phone.

"Well, I think we should call 911!" Zoey said.

"True, but by the time they got us out of here we'd still miss our performance," Chloe reasoned.

"Yeah, the show starts in fifteen minutes," I said, looking at my watch.

"You're right," Zoey conceded. "And it's going to be pretty darn embarrassing when they show up with three police cars, two fire trucks and an ambulance just to unlatch a storage room door. We'll never live it down."

"They'll probably STILL be laughing at us at our high school graduation," Chloe mused. "I'd rather just wait for our moms to get here after the show."

I could NOT believe I had come this far only to be stuck in a storage unit inside the ice arena with the show starting in twelve minutes.

I got a huge lump in my throat thinking about Brandon. Now he was going to have to leave his home and friends at WCD and start over again.

I felt terrible for him. But I was powerless. Signing up for this stupid show was a HUGE mistake.

If only I'd just let MacKenzie skate for Fuzzy Friends like she'd wanted. Then Brandon's life would not have to be turned upside down again. My heart hurt just thinking about the stuff he'd been through.

He had lost his parents, and I totally took mine for granted.

Hot tears began to sting my eyes, but I blinked them back. I heard Chloe and Zoey starting to sniffle too.

Brandon was going to leave just when we were
starting to get to know each other.

Brianna was such a BRAT to him, but he still gave her
that cute thankyou note from the puppies and—

That's when a little lightbulb went on in my brain.

BRIANNA THE BRAT?!

YES! My nutty little sister, who I could always count on to be a total PAIN in the butt.

"Chloe! I've got an idea! Dial my phone number! Quick! Before your phone dies!"

"What? But why?" Chloe asked. "Didn't you leave it in the dressing room? Everyone was supposed to be dressed and cleared out of there thirty minutes ago."

"I know! Just call! PLEASE! We're running out of time! The show starts in ten minutes!"

Chloe and Zoey stared at me like I was nuts.

Finally Chloe shrugged, called my phone and put it on speaker so we all could hear.

It rang once. Twice. Then three times.

I had set it up so that it would go to voicemail on the fifth ring.

"Please answer! Please answer!" I pleaded aloud.

It rang a fourth time. Then . . .

"Hello! Who is this?" said a small, squeaky voice.

OMG! BRIANNA! You have my cell phone?! Thank goodness!

Chloe and Zoey started screaming excitedly too.

"Sorry, but this isn't me," Brianna continued. "I'm not home right now because I'm waiting for Nikki to skate. Please leave a message. Goodbye!"

"NOOO! Don't hang up!!" we all shouted desperately.

"Please, Brianna! Listen to me! Don't hang up!" I begged. "I was just calling to tell you that, um, you can play Princess Sugar Plum on my phone while we're sliding on the ice, okay?"

Long silence. "Really?"

"Really!"

"Goody gumdrops! Can Miss Penelope play too? I told her not to 'borrow' your phone and play the Princess Sugar Plum game, but she did it anyway. It's all HER fault, not mine. But she's very sorry!"

"Sure, Brianna, Miss Penelope can play too."

"Okay! Thanks! BYE!"

"WAIT!!" I screamed. "I need to talk to Mom or Dad! It's an emergency."

"Daddy went to go get me popcorn. And Mom is talking to that lady from ballet class with the big mouth. I'm not supposed to interrupt Mom again, or else. But guess who I see walking by? It's BRANDON THE COOTIE GUY! Hi, Brandon the Cootie Guy! It's me! We talked on the phone, remember?! Nikki was in the shower and that dead squirrel was in Mrs Wallabanger's backyard."

Muffled voices.

I could NOT believe Brianna was telling all of our personal business like that.

"Brianna! BRIANNA!" I yelled.

"WHAAAT!" she huffed.

"Can you give the phone to Brandon the Cootie

Guy? I need to talk to him. Okay?" I said.

"Well, just for a little bit. I'm supposed to be playing Princess Sugar Plum on this phone. Hold on."

More muffled voices.

"Hello, Nikki!"

"Brandon! OMG! We're stuck in a storage locker in the arena! Storage Area C, locker seventeen. Chloe's phone is about to die any minute. Please come get us out!"

"WHAT? Where did you say you were?"

"We're stuck in a—"

That's when the battery died on Chloe's phone and it went dead.

The three of us just sat there in the pitch-dark, stunned and speechless.

We had no idea whether or not Brandon had heard

any of the details about where we were. But just
when we were about to give up hope . . .

The show was starting in four minutes.

We raced back to our dressing room and grabbed our skates and clown wigs, with Brianna tagging along.

Her eyes lit up when she saw the huge, colourful gift-wrapped box. "Nikki, can I have that really big present?"

"No, Brianna, it's empty. That's just a prop for clowns to use."

"I wanna be a clown TOO!" She pouted.

That's when Chloe, Zoey and I got the exact same idea at the exact same moment.

I guess the old saying "Brilliant minds think alike" is true.

The arena was filled to capacity, and the excitement was so electric you could feel it in the air.

Several local television stations were broadcasting live.

Victoria Steel, looking more glam than ever, warmly welcomed the audience and encouraged them to donate generously to the charitable organisations being represented in the show.

Then she made a surprise announcement. "To show our commitment to your community, in addition to the three thousand dollars that each organisation is receiving, *Holiday on Ice* is going to award an additional ten-thousand-dollar cash prize to the crowd favourite."

At that news, the entire audience stood up and cheered like crazy.

Talk about crowd participation!

This was turning into *American Idol.*

On ICE!

The big cash prize sounded exciting and all. And I was sure Fuzzy Friends could use it.

But my personal goal was simply to try to get through the entire routine and perform well enough to be awarded the $3,000.

Soon the lights dimmed and the ice show got under way.

I wasn't the least bit surprised to see that MacKenzie had been selected as the opening act.

She skated to music from *Swan Lake* and was AWESOME!

And when she finished, the audience gave her a standing ovation.

As far as I could tell, MacKenzie was pretty much a major contender for the crowd favourite award. She knew it too, because she kept posing and waving to the audience. . .

When MacKenzie came off the ice, she looked really shocked and surprised to see us in the waiting area backstage.

I smiled and waved, but she just stuck her nose in the air and walked right past us.

"MacKenzie, you're a rotten little sneak. That was a new LOW for you. You've obviously hit rock bottom and started to dig," I said right to her face.

She whipped around and sneered at me. "You say that like it's a bad thing. Actually, I was just trying to do you a favour by saving you and your little friends from public humiliation. But if you insist, go right ahead. LOSERS!"

By the time it was our turn to skate, I was a nervous wreck.

My knees were wobbly even BEFORE I got on the ice.

But somehow I made it into position without falling on my face.

As we waited for the music to start, Zoey gave Chloe and me a big smile.

Then she whispered loudly, "Every human being is a clown but only few have the courage to show it – Charlie Rivel."

I smiled. "Thanks, Zoey!"

OMG! The butterflies in my stomach were so bad I felt like I was going to lose my lunch right on the ice in front of the audience.

That's when Zoey whispered even louder. "A clown is an angel with a red nose – J. T. 'Bubba' Sikes."

I was like, "PUH-LEEZE! Enough already, Zoey. It was cute the first time, but the philosophical CLOWN-ISMS are starting to get on my last nerve!"

But I just said that inside my head, so no one heard it but me.

I knew she was just trying to make me feel better.

I was actually pretty lucky to have a BFF like her.

As the music blared over the speakers, Chloe and Zoey floated across the ice like graceful butterflies.

Okay. Like graceful butterflies wearing stupid clown costumes.

I was supposed to zig, but I zagged.

Or was I supposed to zag, but I zigged?

In any event, I tripped, fell on my butt and slid across the ice at ninety miles per hour like a human bobsled.

Then, *BAM!!* I crashed right into the huge gift we were using as a prop.

Chloe and Zoey looked totally stunned and stopped skating.

I felt so terrible about messing up our routine, I
wanted to cry. MacKenzie was right! All we were
doing was making fools of ourselves.

I half expected to hear Victoria shriek,

"SECURITY! Get those CLOWNS off of my ice!"

And once we were kicked out of the show, Fuzzy Friends would close and Brandon would be forced to move.

I would probably never see him again ☹!

I just sat there stunned, too exhausted to get up.

But that's when I noticed the most amazing thing.

The entire audience was LAUGHING.

And all the little kids were on their feet pointing and clapping.

Apparently, they thought me skidding across the ice

on my behind and almost cracking open my skull was part of a little comedy act or something.

Then it occurred to me that we WERE wearing clown outfits.

DUH!

And clowns were supposed to be funny!

DUH!

And they were always falling on the ground and knocking each other over.

DUH!

I think Chloe and Zoey must have noticed the crowd's reaction and come to the exact same conclusion.

The crowd seemed to LOVE US!!

I mean, REALLY LOVE US!

From that point on, we totally hammed it up.

The crowd went KA-RAY-ZEE when we started doing funky dance steps from our old *Ballet of the Zombies* routine. I'm guessing it was probably because no one had ever seen ZOMBIE CLOWNS do the MOONWALK in ICE SKATES before!

I even threw in a few dance moves from that time Brianna and I performed LIVE at Queasy Cheesy!

I felt so happy and relaxed that, suddenly, skating just wasn't that difficult for me anymore.

It almost seemed to come naturally.

FINALLY!

The strange thing was that I didn't accidentally fall down, not even ONCE, for the entire two and a half minutes that remained.

I only FELL DOWN on PURPOSE!

To make the crowd laugh.

Hey! I was a clown!

It was my JOB!

As our music ended I wanted to keep skating.

This was the most fun Chloe, Zoey and I had ever had together.

But there's more!

The crowd got an unexpected surprise when a tiny little clown popped out like a demented jack-in-the-box. . .

BRIANNA!!!

I guess you could say she stole the show. . .

We totally nailed that last pose, and the audience went WILD!! And we received a standing ovation.

After we got off the ice, we were SO happy! We did a group hug with Brianna and Miss Penelope!

I didn't think our day could get any better, but it did. Guess who won audience favourite and a cheque for $10,000 for Fuzzy Friends!

PAY TO THE
ORDER OF: ⌇⌇⌇⌇⌇ ~ ~ |$10,000.00
TEN THOUSAND DOLLARS

The whole time we were getting our picture taken, MacKenzie was glaring at me.

I wanted to walk up to her and say, "Hey, what's WRONG? You MAD, girlfriend? Huh? Is that it? You MAD?!!"

But I didn't. Because *I* was trying to be nice and show good sportsmanship.

In spite of the fact that *SHE* was the biggest CHEATER on the planet!!

I couldn't believe she stole our costumes AND locked us in that storage room.

But her evil little plan totally BACKFIRED on her.

CLOWNS knocking each other over and sliding around on their butts is really FUNNY stuff.

But prissy Sugar Plum Fairies doing the same thing? Not so much!

Just as I was coming off the ice, I saw Brandon, and he looked SO happy.

I almost DIED when he handed me a beautiful bouquet of flowers.

"Congratulations, Nikki!" Brandon said.

"Thanks, Brandon! This whole thing has been unbelievable."

"I heard there was a mix-up with your costumes too. But I knew you'd be okay. You guys totally rocked the ice!"

"Well, it was worth it. I'm just happy we were able to keep Fuzzy Friends open so that your gran — er, I mean Betty — can continue to take care of those animals," I said, and plastered a big, dopey grin across my face.

But deep down inside I cringed and wanted to kick myself for almost referring to Betty as Brandon's grandmother.

It's weird, but the more I've got to know Brandon, the MORE questions I have about who he really is. And the LAST thing he needs right now is some busybody snooping into his personal business and gossiping behind his back.

I've personally lived through that with Miss Motormouth MacKenzie, and it's been TORTURE.

So for now, I know all I need to know — that Brandon is an AMAZING friend who's always there when I need him. And I'm happy I was able to be there for him too.

I hugged my bouquet of roses and buried my face in them.

I inhaled their sweet, romantic fragrance, awed by how much they smelled like perfumey . . . um . . . roses.

"Well, thank you for all your help. Nikki, you're . . . AWESOME!" Brandon gushed.

I blushed profusely.

Then he gave me a big hug!

OMG! I thought I was going to pee my pants.

BRANDON. ACTUALLY. HUGGED. ME!!

SQUEEEEEEEE!!!

But now I'm even more CONFUSED!

Because I don't know if it was a . . .

"You're my FRIEND" hug.

Or a "You're my really GOOD friend" hug!

Or a "You're MORE than a good friend" hug!!

Or a "You're my GIRLFRIEND" hug!!!

I really want to ask him.

But I can't!

Because THEN he'll know . . .

I really want to KNOW!

And him knowing all of this would just make me supernervous.

Which sounds really crazy.

Right?

Sorry, I can't help it.

I'M SUCH A DORK!!!
☺!!

Don't miss more diaries

Dork Diaries

Dork Diaries: Party Time

Dork Diaries: Pop Star

Dork Diaries: Skating Sensation

Dork Diaries: Dear Dork

Dork Diaries: Holiday Heartbrea

by Rachel Renée Russell!

MOST IMPORTANT TIP EVER FROM NIKKI MAXWELL:

Always let your inner **DORK** shine through!

#1 New York Times Bestselling Series

**Dork Diaries:
TV Star**

**Dork Diaries:
Once Upon a Dork**

**Dork Diaries:
Drama Queen**

**Dork Diaries:
Puppy Love**

**Dork Diaries:
OMG! All About
Me Diary**

**Dork Diaries:
How to Dork
Your Diary**

Do you love

DORK
diaries

and reading all about Nikki's
not-so-fabulous life??

Then don't miss out on the
BRAND NEW series from
Rachel Renée Russell!
featuring new dork on the block,

**MAX
CRUMBLY!**

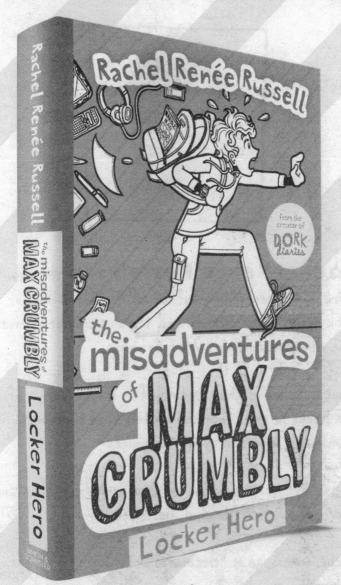

Rachel Renée Russell

the misadventures of **MAX CRUMBLY**

Locker Hero

from the creator of DORK diaries

the misadventures of **MAX CRUMBLY**

Locker Hero

SIMON & SCHUSTER

"If you like Tom Gates, Diary of A Wimpy Kid and, of course, Dork Diaries you'll love this!" *The Sun*

Rachel Renée Russell is the #1 *New York Times* bestselling author of the block-buster book series Dork Diaries and the exciting new series The Misadventures of Max Crumbly.

There are more than twenty-five million copies of her books in print worldwide, and they have been translated into thirty-six languages.

She enjoys working with her two daughters, Erin and Nikki, who help write and illustrate her books.

Rachel's message is "Become the hero you've always admired!"